Sometime Yesterday

SOMETIME YESTERDAY

by

Yvonne Heidt

2012

SOMETIME YESTERDAY

ISBN 10: 1-60282-680-3
ISBN 13: 978-1-60282-680-9

This Trade Paperback Original Is Published By
Bold Strokes Books, Inc.
P.O. Box 249
Valley Falls, NY 12185

First Edition: August 2012

Credits
Editor: Cindy Cresap
Production Design: Susan Ramundo
Cover Design By Sheri (graphicartist2020@hotmail.com)

Acknowledgments

Thank you. Those two words don't seem nearly enough for the appreciation I hold for the wonderful people at Bold Strokes Books. Radclyffe, I will always be grateful for the chance you took on me and the wonderful opportunity I received from Jennifer Knight to be included in the NADF.

For the amazing Victoria Oldham, who gets me and always knows which button to push to make it all better. Without your encouraging words and understanding of my little quirks, I wouldn't have come this far. I appreciate you.

As my senior editor, Cindy Cresap deserves a medal, really. I am grateful for the time and expertise you put into this story. It's a fine art form to teach with patience and humor. All of my hair has grown back; how about yours?

Maralee Lackman, my BFF—who literally saved my life. Thank you for loving and believing in me.

Shelia Powell for the gifts you gave me. My personal journey is forever changed by the experience.

I would also like to thank my very first readers—Melody Starkey and Paris Honsowetz, who loved my story and hounded me for more. Without you, I would have never finished *Sometime Yesterday*.

Special love and thanks to Mom and Papa, for never giving up on me, even when you should have. Unconditional love and gratitude goes to my living children, Kerri-Ann and Daniel, who deserve much more than I could ever possibly give them in this lifetime.

Sandy—thank you for loving me unconditionally through all of life's twists and turns. What a ride the last eleven years has been!

Dedication

For Deserae Marie
My beautiful daughter
Who sends me love on the delicate wings of butterflies

“That which is dreamed, cannot be lost,
cannot be undreamed.”

The Sandman

Chapter One

Good-bye, old friend. I know I said I would love you forever. Natalie Chambers took one last look around the Tudor house she and her very recent ex-husband had shared. The movers had been in earlier and had taken all the furniture and boxes that she carefully tagged. Jason and his new wife, Tracy, would be back from their honeymoon at the end of the week. The only thing left to do here was say good-bye. She pulled on her coat, grabbed her keys, and leaned into the doorframe for a moment.

Natalie almost couldn't blame him for being attracted to the beautiful coed. Almost. Tracy Chambers was everything Natalie wasn't. Tall. Blond. Thin. Oh, and let's not forget young, pregnant, and married to the man Natalie had expected to spend her life with. She locked the door and gave it one last loving pat. *I'm so sorry that forever turned out to be twelve years and a generous divorce settlement. If it's any consolation, House, I will miss you more than I will him.* Natalie was surprised at that. Somehow, she thought she should hurt more or feel something, anything. Instead, she felt strangely relieved that this awkward and completely disappointing period in her life was over.

With her arms crossed against the wind, Natalie flipped her long ponytail out of her coat, wiped her tears with her sleeve, and walked to her car. She was ready to head into her new life.

❖

Late that night, Natalie pulled into her new driveway. It looked different in the dark but she still remembered how charmed she was by the pink four and a half bedroom house. She instantly fell in love with the hardwood floors and little nooks. She'd thought perhaps here she could finally find her fairy tale. When she entered the third floor turret room that overlooked the Pacific Ocean, she was sold. Natalie smelled the salty air and could easily imagine that on a windy day she could feel its misty spray. It would make a perfect studio for her painting.

She also recalled how shocked the real estate agent looked when Natalie made an offer on the spot. She was surprised at that herself. She'd never done anything so impulsive in her life.

While Natalie stretched her stiff legs and back from the long car ride, she caught a movement from the second floor window. She stared harder and thought she saw the curtains move. Great, she'd been here two minutes and was already seeing ghosts. She was tired, not seeing things.

Natalie felt a pulse of fear as she inserted her key. There was a face staring back at her. She giggled when she realized it was her own reflection and let herself in. "Hey, honey. I'm home." She called out in the foyer.

She was excited to finally see the furniture she had ordered online since the purchase of her house. She'd spent many hours on the phone with her best friend, Mary, deciding which piece went where. Now that she was exploring the first floor, she already felt like she belonged here. She stopped in the living room.

Hanging above the fireplace was an old oil portrait. Natalie rubbed her upper arms in an attempt to warm them from the chill that followed her inside and stepped closer. God, the woman gazing from the oversized canvas was gorgeous. She stood in profile, looking out a window. Tall and slender, she had one hand gracefully on the window frame and the other resting on the back of a chair. Natalie frowned. Something about her seemed familiar. Her long, dark hair fell loosely in thick curls to her waist and she wore what appeared to be a flowing nightgown. The glow of the moon outside the window made the material semi-transparent, outlining the swell of her breasts and her tiny waist. Her legs and feet were blocked by the chair. Natalie could see the woman's individual eyelashes and the flush of her cheek. Her red mouth was set softly as if she were blowing a kiss to someone, perhaps her lover, standing beyond the frame. Whoever had painted this woman was completely enchanted with her. The attention to detail spoke of a woman cherished, a feeling Natalie had been waiting for most of her adult life. She checked for the artist's signature, but it must have been covered by the heavy, ornate frame.

She was sure the painting hadn't been in the house when she first viewed it with the realtor, nor did she remember purchasing it. The room was cold and Natalie rubbed her arms against the chill. She would have to ask Mary where it came from.

Meanwhile, she needed to find the thermostat and start unpacking the few possessions she'd brought with her. Even in the short time she allotted herself, Natalie was super organized. The car didn't hold much of her former life. A small suitcase that held enough clothes until the movers arrived, a train case full of her makeup and toiletries, some jewelry that her mother had given her, and pictures of her family. Her art collection would arrive later in the week. She refused to leave one painting for the newly wedded couple to enjoy.

Natalie paused to admire the workmanship that created the slender curved staircase. She loved the details in this house, the intricate Victorian molding near the arched cathedral ceilings, the restored walnut woodwork that framed all the built-in bookshelves and graced every doorframe. She was elated to find intact beautiful stained glass windows throughout the house. She knew that in a very short time she would be able to make the house feel like her own.

Natalie caressed the glossy wood railing as she climbed the stairs. The large master bedroom was at the end of the hall. The previous owners had knocked out a wall of an adjoining bedroom to add more space and a luxurious master bath. Natalie could feel a breeze from beneath the door. She stepped into the room and found the front window wide open. Funny, she hadn't noticed the window open when she stood outside. She took in the breathless ocean view.

It was just past sunset with dark purple streaks in the sky, and blue twilight undulated on the ocean's rolling surface. The waves were peaceful in their endless motion. She searched for the first star and made a wish. The very first of her brand new life. Natalie double-checked the latch before going back downstairs.

❖

After unpacking the trunk and backseat of her car, Natalie stopped in the kitchen to grab a bottle of water and see what Mary had stocked the refrigerator and cabinets with earlier that week. Natalie knew Mary wanted to make sure that the divorce and the move were as smooth as she could possibly make it. They had always had keys to each other's houses until Mary had relocated to Bayside a couple of years ago. It was Natalie's main reason for moving here. She was happy that once again, she would live in the same town as Mary and was looking forward to her help, and her company, in the morning.

She put her empty bottle of water on the counter and turned toward the hallway. As she rounded the corner to the stairs, she felt something brush against her.

Was that a spider web? God, she hated bugs. Natalie jumped and waved her arms. Skin crawling, she took to the stairs double-time; shaking her hair out to make sure nothing was stuck in it. When she reached the bedroom, she stared at the door, apprehension snaking its way to the base of her spine. It was closed. She was almost certain she'd left it open. She reached for the knob, but before she could touch it, the door swung away from her as though opened from the other side.

Natalie felt herself chill to the bone. Arms folded over her chest, she crossed the threshold. The room was freezing. The window she'd closed an hour earlier was open again, the long drapes blowing into the room. A faint scent of lavender hung in the cold air. Natalie ran over to the window and shut it. The wind must have blown the door shut.

Natalie entered her large bathroom. Now here was a modern slice of heaven. Sandstone colored marble covered the countertops and floor, matching the bronze towel rings and faucets. The deep corner tub was gleaming yet looked bare. Natalie looked forward to adding some personal touches with plants and colorful girlie bottles and jars. The scent of lavender was stronger in here. She wondered if the previous owner left a candle or perhaps some potpourri in the linen closet. After a quick search, she didn't find anything and gave up. She was simply too tired to care at the moment. She pulled out a couple of towels and crossed to the tub. As soon as she opened the faucets, water came flowing out of a majestic lion's open mouth. Jet streams built into the side shot more hot water into the tub. While her bath was running, Natalie went back into the bedroom and found the nightgown buried in her suitcase. As she undressed, she watched the window, half-expecting to see it rattle loose and creak open again. She chuckled to herself, trying to put her jitters into perspective. She clearly needed to adjust to living alone. This was a new place. Once she got to know it, she wouldn't jump at every noise.

She strolled back into the bathroom and stood in front of the wall-to-wall mirror, inspecting her weary face. The furrow between her eyebrows and stress lines bracketing her mouth were evidence of sleepless nights and the pain of divorce. Natalie made a firm decision to stop thinking of herself as a victim. The worst was behind her and she could be proud of herself that she didn't leave frozen shrimp in the hollow drapery rods as a parting shot to her ex-husband and his new wife.

At least the split from Jason took care of that last fifteen pounds she'd been trying to lose for the past few years. She stood at five foot-nothing-tall and every pound on her small frame counted.

The mirror fogged with steam from the running bath. From her peripheral vision, she saw something move behind her. She spun around quickly, but the shadow was gone. She noticed her hand tremble slightly when she wiped the condensation away and peeked again. Nothing. Natalie sighed. She reminded herself she was tired, not hallucinating. She turned off the water and slipped into the tub. Perfect. She could literally feel the stress lifting as she washed her hair then lay back on the built-in seat and closed her eyes. Soothed by the heat and weightlessness, she let the long, emotional day soak off.

Natalie let her mind drift. It occurred to her that this would be the first time in her life she would be living alone. She went from her parents to the college dorm and then on to Jason. Although, living with Jason the past couple of years had been like living alone. She tried not to dwell on regrets. Her thoughts didn't land on any one particular thing for long. Like butterflies, they flitted toward a memory, retreated, and went on to the next.

CRASH.

Natalie's start of surprise almost propelled her from the bath. Her eyes popped open and she quickly planted her feet to brace herself. *What was that?* She realized she must have fallen asleep because the water was ice cold. She strained to hear the sound again, but all she could hear was her own heart beat in her ears.

Natalie wrapped herself in a towel and approached the bathroom door. She slowly turned the knob, holding it in a death grip, ready to slam it closed if anything was on the other side. *Steady, girl, it's just an old house making old house noises.* She took a deep breath and stepped out into the bedroom. After checking the window and the ones adjoining it, she didn't see anything amiss that could warrant such a loud noise. She cautiously stepped into the hallway, pressing herself against the wall to step sideways into the adjoining guest room. She couldn't see anything out of place and that window was also latched tight.

Natalie retreated to her bedroom and put her nightgown on. She'd have to check the yard in the morning to see if a there was a loose shed door or something. A brand new bed had been delivered earlier in the week and Mary, being the friend that she was, had it made and ready for her. She even had the pretty sheets turned down. As Natalie slid beneath the covers, she felt some regret for the beautiful antique four-poster she'd left behind at her old house. On the other hand, she thought, there was a great deal of disappointment attached to that particular bed. Disappointments better left in her old life. Besides, she'd be damned if she was going to bring any part of Jason into her new space or allow his memories in her new bedroom. Instead, she could look forward to finding local antique shops and auctions to find new treasures.

Natalie turned out the bedside lamp and tried to go to sleep. It was during this in-between time of awareness and floating off to a dream that Natalie's insecurities slapped at her. What was wrong with her? Would she be able to manage a new life alone? She was in her thirties, loved her painting, and was healthy. But was she so difficult to love?

❖

The gentle rocking motion of a hammock combined with the smell of sweet summer sunshine, filled Natalie's senses as dust motes floated lazily in the air. She had never felt so relaxed in her life. No, that wasn't right. She had never felt so serene. She heard soft laughter behind her. It was gentle and feminine. She tried to move her head to see who it was, but she couldn't.

"You came back," she said. "I knew you would come."

"Pardon me?"

"You're here. I've been waiting so long."

She felt the woman move directly behind her and continue to push the hammock while humming softly. Natalie didn't recognize the song, both haunting and melodic at once, but it soothed her like a lullaby and she floated back to sleep. The sun disappeared as a cloud drifted in front of it. Rain started to fall in cold, heavy drops. Natalie struggled to move, tangled in the hammock, and fell to the ground. Thunder clapped in the sky.

"He's here! Go back, dear heart. *Now!*"

❖

Natalie gasped and sat straight up in bed, her breath coming in short bursts. She couldn't find her bearings and fought not to panic. Outside, the storm raged. Rain pelted the windows and the room illuminated with a flash of lightning. Natalie covered her head with the blankets and tried to go back to sleep, humming the melody she'd never heard outside her dream. As she drifted, she thought she felt a hand gently smooth her shoulder and she shivered. Over the noise of the storm's crescendo, she heard a soft whisper.

"*Shhh. Sleep, my angel. I'll watch over you.*"

CHAPTER TWO

The next time Natalie opened her eyes, it was to rays of bright sunshine streaming in through a crack in the drapes. She felt as if she should be remembering something important, but the sensation danced around on the edge of her consciousness.

She threw open the drapes and rubbed her eyes. There was no sign of rain. The birds were chirping and the sky still fairly pink and orange from the sunrise. Vaguely, she wondered why she thought it was raining. Natalie quickly made the bed and ran into the bathroom to wash her face and brush her teeth. She was excited to start the day and see Mary.

The odd feeling she had woken with disappeared as she took stock of the house, *her* house. Once again, she was grateful for Mary, this time for the coffee pot sitting on the kitchen counter and fresh coffee in the freezer. A beautiful arched stone fireplace stood sentry in the room, the red polished brick scrubbed immaculate. The kitchen had been beautifully remodeled. Come to think of it, the whole place looked wonderful. Natalie wondered why the previous owners decided to sell after putting in so much work. The purchase price certainly didn't reflect the apparent cost of the renovations.

The cabinets were obviously original but restored to match the golden oak floor. Granite counters and the stainless steel appliances gleamed in the morning light streaming through a large window over the farmhouse sink. It wasn't true to the style of the period, but who really wanted a closet sized Victorian kitchen anyway? Natalie appreciated the modern conveniences.

While she was waiting for the coffee to brew, she looked out the back door to survey the rear property. She couldn't help but sigh when she saw how derelict and overgrown it appeared. Tall grass, weeds, and blackberry bushes grew wild, turning what must have been beautiful plant beds and orderly walkways into a playground of disorder. It would be a huge project, but her hands itched to get in the dirt. The rich smell of the earth and the feeling of accomplishment she compared to the process of painting. The art of creation fulfilled her in much the same way. She wondered who would be tending her gardens at her previous house this year and felt a little homesick.

Natalie poured herself a cup of coffee and sat at the solid oak table. She dug in her purse for a notebook and pen to start a new list.

She was overwhelmed and inexplicably, she began to cry. She'd kept herself so busy over the last few months, she hadn't had time to breathe, let alone think. Tears landed on her list and made tiny circles in the letters, rendering some of the items illegible. She had hardly expected to be starting her life over at thirty-two. As far as she'd been concerned, the last twelve years hadn't been all bad. Well, except for one detail. Natalie had never felt any passion toward Jason. None. She knew the problem lay with her. Jason was always ready, and over the years, she'd come to dread "that" look.

Natalie winced when she recalled the first time Jason had called her frigid. Then there was the humiliating experience with the sex therapist. It was his idea, of course. Natalie gave her ex-husband props; he'd tried everything in the book to get her to respond.

She admitted the fault was her own and put all of her insecurity into her paintings. She tucked her fantasies of happy-ever-after away and settled.

She ripped out the shopping list and reminded herself that she could have new dreams now, and she had plenty to look forward to. Room by room, Natalie took inventory of what was in the house, what was coming, and what she would need in order to complete each room to her satisfaction. She finished her tour in the living room. Pausing before the painting above the fireplace, she tilted her head to the side and stared. The painting looked different. Natalie could have sworn that the woman had been standing completely in profile. This morning, she was looking over her shoulder and smiling shyly, her soft brown eyes curtained by the fall of her dark hair. Natalie backed away and studied the subject from different angles. The artist in her appreciated the detail and subtle colors that brought a dreamy quality to the painting. The woman was so beautiful, and yet again, Natalie had the odd feeling she had seen her somewhere before. She traced her fingers along the woman's hair to her waist. When she caught herself wondering how soft the woman's skin was, she quickly dropped her hand and stood back. She told herself that she was simply exhausted, not losing her mind. The painting hadn't changed; that would be impossible.

She yelped and jumped about two feet when the doorbell rang. Through the pane of glass in the door, she could see Mary standing on the porch. Natalie laughed and quickly let her in.

"That doorbell is so loud, you about stopped my heart." They embraced and she grabbed Mary's hand and dragged her toward the kitchen. "You look awesome." Natalie said and meant it. Mary Chapman had perfected her version of the California casual look. Streaked blond hair swung at the tips of her shoulders, she had cheerful cornflower blue eyes, and easy warmth lit her face. She left her designer suits in San Francisco when she and her family relocated to Bayside, but they were replaced with equally designer jeans that hugged her hips and flared fashionably at her feet.

"Slow down, Nat. I've been here, remember?"

"About that, how fricking cool are you? Thank you so much for getting the place ready for me." Natalie poured a cup of coffee and got the creamer out of the fridge. "I see you even stocked *your* stuff."

Mary laughed. "Well, I knew I'd be here all the time. It's so good to have you close. Look out, Bayside, the terrible duo is together again!" She lifted her coffee cup in a toast.

"How are you feeling?"

"Like I've been dropped into a different life."

"I know it hurts, honey." Mary patted her hand gently. "But I can't say I'm sorry you left the jerk and moved here. I've missed you terribly. Do you want to talk about it?"

Natalie waved off the question. "Absolutely not. No sad talk today. We have work to do. By the way, where did that painting come from over the fireplace? Did you buy it?"

"Nuh uh. It was here when I started getting the place ready."

"I'll have to ask the real estate agent then. If I'm not mistaken, I hear the moving truck. Let's roll, buddy."

Six hours later, with the movers finished and gone, the afternoon found them sitting on a dark gray, low back sectional couch in the corner of the parlor with their feet on boxes.

"God," Natalie said, "I feel like that truck ran me over before it left."

"That's because we worked our asses off."

"I wish I had some champagne."

Mary blew her bangs out of her eyes. "You do, Nat. Bottom shelf in the fridge."

"Well, shit, what are we sitting here for?"

Laughing, they ran into the kitchen and popped the cork on the Dom Pérignon Mary had left chilling for their reunion.

After toasting Natalie's new life in the house, Mary gave her a hug. "I have to go get the kids, and it just wouldn't do to have Mommy reeking of alcohol in the afternoon. Now that they're teenagers, they would never let me live it down." She looked at Natalie hopefully. "Maybe you could come over and have dinner with us?"

Natalie briefly thought about how great it would be to see the kids and Mary's husband, Steve. They were her second family. Then the thought came that she just couldn't stomach the pity. Well intentioned as it may be, she didn't want to talk about the divorce or how she was feeling. She just wanted to move past it.

"I would love to take a rain check on that," Natalie said. "I'm not ready to face everyone yet."

"Okay, Nat." Mary hugged her good-bye. "I love you."

"I love you, too. Thank you so much for everything. " Natalie was grateful that Mary let her refusal stand so easily and didn't try to persuade her.

She stood in the doorway watching Mary's car go back toward the town of Bayside and out of sight. She looked at her watch. Her back was sore and she was tired, but it was still early afternoon and she should head into town herself. She had a long list of things to buy. Natalie jumped when a door slammed shut somewhere in the house. Her nerves came back to greet her. Her fear the night before had seemed silly in the light of day, but now that she was here alone again, she was a little jumpy.

This is ridiculous. Natalie chided herself, squared her shoulders, and marched to the stairs with determination. She would *not* be scared in her own house. When she reached the landing, she looked along the hall to see which door could have made the noise.

They were closed, every single one of them.

Natalie felt the hair on her neck rise. Goose bumps prickled her skin. Obviously, with all the windows and doors open, something was bound to slam. She checked every room, shut each window, and made sure she left every door open. Nothing spooky jumped out at her. When she was done, she washed her hands, changed her dusty clothes, then gathered her purse and went out to her car. As she slid the key into the ignition, she made sure to look and see if the window to her bedroom was closed. It was. She quickly backed out of the driveway and headed to town, dismayed to have a sense of relief at leaving her new home for a little while.

❖

Natalie opened her window to let in the sea air while she was driving. The coast was beautiful. The highway hugged the cliff, and to her right was nothing but the ocean. The view of the water was broken with white caps and several large rocks that jutted out in between the waves. She loved the water and always had. The notes and melodies in the eighties music playing on the radio sang to her soul and reminded her of her younger years when her dreams reached to the sky and anything was possible. She spied a bald eagle as he tipped his wings to fly over the cliff. And that, at least, was a good omen. She adjusted the radio and beat the steering wheel in time while singing her favorite Bon Jovi song.

At the next turn in the road, she could see the town nestled in the small valley. When she got closer, she let out a happy sound. It was beautiful with wide, clean streets. A small church spire rose in the air next to an idyllic park where children were playing. The yards all looked manicured and well cared for; colorful flowers spilled out of porch pots and lawn borders. It was postcard perfect and she already felt a sense of pride that she belonged here now.

Natalie turned left on to Main Street. *How quaint is that?* She followed it to the hardware slash home store on the corner and pulled her little red Mercedes into the lot. Half the stuff on her list could be found here, and the other half at Samson's, the local general store on Cedar Street, two blocks away.

She pushed her cart through the immaculate aisles and quickly filled it with odds and ends, making sure to choose a new latch for her bedroom window. The elderly man behind the counter introduced himself.

"Well, hello. Here's a new face." He thrust his hand over the counter to shake Natalie's. "I'm Stan and this is my store."

"It's nice to meet you, Stan. My name is Natalie and I am a new face. I just moved here, yesterday."

Stan ran her items over the scanner and placed them in bags. "Oh, yeah? Which house, if you don't mind me asking? You know these small towns." He gave her a playful wink. "Always gossiping and knowing all your business. I need some new tidbits to share with the boys at the poker game tonight."

Natalie smiled and instantly liked him. "It's the pink Victorian on the cliffs overlooking the ocean. Do you know it?"

His face went dark and his mouth set in a grim line. "The old Seeley place? Yeah, I know it."

Natalie was surprised at how quickly his mood changed. "Is that who owned it?"

"Karen Small didn't tell you about that house before you bought it?" He shook his head and picked up her bags. "Do you need help out with these?" Not waiting for her answer, he barreled out the door to her car.

Natalie rushed over to unlock the trunk. "Is there something I should know, Stan?" She gave a nervous laugh. "What, were there people murdered there or something?"

"Miss Natalie, what's done is done. You own the house, and you should know its history. There's a lot of folk here be willing to tell you all about the old Seeley place and you're likely to get just as many very different stories. But you get your own answers, hear? Give Karen a call and ask her." Stan shut her trunk. "Now then, it was very nice to meet you and I'll be sure to tell the boys tonight that we have a pretty new resident. You need anything, you give me a holler."

Before Natalie could say a word, he nudged her toward the car and went back into the store.

Natalie sat in her car for a moment then dialed Mary's phone.

"My house has a history," she blurted the second she heard her voice. "How come you didn't tell me my house had a history?"

"The house is a hundred years old, Nat. Of course it has a history."

"Well, Stan, the guy who owns the hardware store? He practically crossed himself and threw salt over his shoulder when I told him where I lived. What's up with that?"

She heard Mary's heavy sigh before she answered. "Okay, I should have told you, but you only called me after you'd already written the check, remember?" There was a slight pause. "Rumor has it the house is haunted."

Natalie felt both nauseous and vindicated. She knew there was something strange going on. "Whole story. Spill it, girl."

"You don't really believe in ghosts, do you?"

Natalie rolled her eyes at the hopeful tone in Mary's voice. "Hel-lo, have you met my mother the witch?"

"You know, not to change the subject or anything, but I've never understood that. How come you went to Catholic school?"

Natalie chuckled. "We Irish like to cover all our bases." She heard a loud crash on the other end of the line and the boys screaming in the background.

"Gotta go, Nat. I'll call you back."

The line went dead. Her lovely house had a haunted history. *Crap. Now what?*

Natalie flipped her phone shut and pulled out of the store's parking lot. She turned right at the stop sign and continued on to the grocery store.

Chapter Three

Van Easton lowered her sunglasses so she could better appreciate the sight of the trim figure bent over the trunk of a sporty little car. *Nice pockets.* She caught a glimpse of red hair as the owner sped out of the grocery store parking lot. *And the car ain't bad either.* She grinned and slid the case of water into the bed of her truck and headed back to work. She would be putting in some more late hours as the opening madness of the spring rush would be in less than a month.

She was dog-tired but felt her chest fill with pride at the first sight of the business she co-owned and worked with her father. Set back from the highway, V & V Landscaping was her baby. Since she was added to the letterhead, so to speak, the company had grown from the nursery to include landscaping and custom designs, her specialty.

She flipped the radio off and could hear her tires crunching along the long gravel driveway until she pulled into the side parking lot. She absently waved to a customer who was leaving.

More by habit than anything else, she stopped to straighten a few of the flat carts that were crooked and flashed on a memory of her father handing her a shiny quarter to make sure they were all lined up like little soldiers in formation. The main building was a white two-story farmhouse her parents had converted years ago. She paused at the bottom of the low, wide ramp. Her father had been busy. Large cement planters flanked the railing and burst with riots of colorful violas and purple faced pansies. Red geraniums hung from the overhang of the large porch. She noticed a pretty new fairy wind chime with cobalt wings dancing in the breeze and ringing merrily.

Dad's rocker was empty, as were the other rocking chairs on the porch that usually held one or two of his retired buddies. She glanced at her watch, noticing it was much later than she originally thought. She entered the front door and was struck with a sense of home. For a moment, she could almost see her mother on the other side of the old wood counter, polishing it with loving hands, smiling at her.

The illusion shattered when Jenny, the cashier, greeted her.

"Working tonight, boss?"

"I'm sorry, what did you say?"

"Um, Van? It's closing time. Are you okay?"

She nodded and managed to find her voice. "Go ahead and finish, Jen. I'll see you tomorrow."

Van intended to go to her office but instead turned right at the stairs to the second floor, where she had grown up and her father still lived. She ran her hand lovingly along the smooth banister and saw herself, a young girl, sliding down it.

What was with her tonight? She rolled her shoulders and tried to free herself of the melancholy, yet it followed her up the stairs.

The living room still held traces of her mother, dead now over a decade, but present throughout in the sweet, simple touches scattered throughout the house. There, a colorful afghan folded over the couch and here, a cheerful teapot collection.

Memories of another loss closed her throat and she immediately cut them off. She wasn't going to go there tonight.

"Vannie?" her father called from the kitchen. "Is that you?"

She found him making snack platters. "Poker tonight, Pop?"

He nodded and grinned. "Yep. The boys will be here soon. Wanna stay and see if you can double your paycheck?"

"Not with you, old man, you cheat. Besides, I write the payroll now."

He laughed and turned to wash his hands in the sink. Van noticed how stooped his once broad shoulders had become.

"Did you finish the Whitney job today?"

"Yes, and thank God for it." She grabbed a beer. "If that harpy wanted us to change six things, she wanted us to change a half dozen of another."

He patted her shoulder. "Now, Vannie, Stella Whitney isn't that bad."

Van turned her chair sideways from the table so she could stretch her denim clad legs out and debated whether she should tell him about Ms. Whitney offering her silicone inflated double Ds as a bonus to the final check she was writing. It had been a sticky, ha-ha situation, and Van considered herself lucky she got out with the payment and a pretty harmless pinch on the ass. Instead, she lifted her beer and mumbled, "Mmm," figuring her dad didn't need to know that bit of gossip. She gave him a brief rundown of what else was scheduled that week and then tossed her empty bottle into the recycling bin. "I'll leave you to your game, Dad. I'm going out for a while."

Once out on the highway, she passed the turn to her house and continued to her favorite bar. She felt uneasy and kept checking her rearview mirror. When she reached the door, she turned to look over her shoulder. There was nothing there, but the feeling of being watched stayed with her all night.

Natalie barely noticed the view as she drove home. Her thoughts kept going back to the fact that her house was haunted. No wonder that real estate agent was so happy and pushed everything through so fast. Sneaky broad. One of the first things she was going to do when she got back was call her mother. She hadn't talked to her much since the divorce, not that her mother didn't try. Even though Jason was the one who cheated and left her, Natalie still felt ashamed.

Well, for good or for bad, as Stan had said, the house was hers and she couldn't give it back.

Her mind was racing a mile a minute and Natalie slowed as she took the last bend in the road before turning off. Coasting the driveway toward her *haunted* house, she looked up.

The bedroom window was open. *This sucks*.

Her car was full. Natalie dragged the bags to the front porch before she unlocked the door. She repeated the process to get them just inside the door. She stood in the foyer with her purchases and shut the door.

She looked around carefully. Nothing seemed to be disturbed. With the late afternoon sun streaming into the kitchen, it was hard to believe anything spooky was going on. Maybe she was wrong? Even as she asked herself the question, she knew she couldn't explain the strange situation. As she unpacked her groceries, Natalie made a mental note to call Karen Small first thing in the morning and then sat at the table to call her mom. She twitched when the cell phone rang in her pocket just as she was reaching for it. She looked at the caller ID and grinned.

"Hi, Mom. I was just going to call you."

"I know, dear. That's why I called you first. What's the matter?"

"What makes you think there's something the matter?" Natalie didn't bother waiting for the answer. Her mother always knew when something was wrong, even if she chose not to say so. She usually waited for Natalie to discuss her problems when she was ready. "Evidently, my new house has other residents besides myself, and they are not of the earthbound variety."

"Do you want me to come?"

"Would you, Mom? I know that you planned on coming during the summer, but you're so much better at dealing with this paranormal stuff than I am."

She explained what had happened the night before as well as the day's disturbing events of slamming doors and windows.

Colleen O'Donnell-James was very quiet for a moment. "It's an old house, Nat."

"I know that, Mom."

"I'll call you right back. I have to talk to your father and check on airline tickets." Her mother clicked off without saying good-bye.

Natalie looked out the kitchen window. She blinked and then rubbed her eyes. The garden was beautiful. It was no longer overgrown and patchy. Lush, green lawn spread from the back porch to the cliff. Amongst the flower beds and neat little paths, she could see a white hammock swinging gently in the breeze. A yellow butterfly circled lazily in the afternoon sun. She ran to the back door and opened it.

Only thick, dead grass and a couple of trees stood where she had seen the hammock moments before. She slammed the back door and sprinted back to the window. The pretty garden had disappeared.

Wow. Her imagination was working overtime. It had to be all the talk of ghosts. She shook off the feeling of uncertainty starting in her stomach and turned her attention to unpacking. Natalie went back to the foyer to drag the rest of her bags in. Some were going upstairs and some were going to the basement. Though she knew she wasn't going anywhere near it, until her mother arrived. Not after the talk of spirits. Some things you just never outgrew, and her fear of basements seemed to be one of them. She stepped carefully around the boxes in the front room. The movers had left the furniture somewhat in the areas she pointed out to them. Mary could help her organize the rest.

Natalie looked at the painting apprehensively. The woman was still looking sideways. No changes there.

Her phone rang again in the kitchen. By the time she got there, it had already gone to voice mail. It was her mother. She was arriving in three days, on Friday afternoon, and renting a car. Natalie was thankful they all seemed to come equipped with GPS these days; otherwise her mother would never find the house. Natalie heated a frozen dinner and ate in the silent room, thinking she had to find her stereo, since it was far too quiet in the house. She needed the background noise. She wished that Mary would call her back and she reached for the phone to call her instead. The battery indicator had no bars. She searched her purse but her phone charger wasn't in it.

Natalie finally went upstairs. She was relieved to find the doors were open as she'd left them and marched deliberately into her room.

Shadows were filling the corners while the sun faded and the night was getting cold. She closed the window and spun around to face the room. Other than once again smelling lavender in the air, she couldn't feel anything off. Natalie crossed to her suitcase and searched for the charger. It wasn't there either, but she was certain she'd packed it. She dumped the bag out onto the bed. It was gone.

Great. She was alone, in a supposedly haunted house.

With a dead phone.

CHAPTER FOUR

Welcome.

Natalie dripped water on the floor and stared at the word written in the steam on the mirror then cleaned off the writing with her towel, telling herself it must have been there before and she just didn't notice it the night her bath went cold, since there was no steam left by the time she had gotten out. She blamed the doodle on the previous owner. Fingerprint drawings could last for a long time on a surface that hadn't been cleaned, right?

"Are you awake yet?" Mary called from downstairs, scaring her half to death. "It's eight thirty."

Natalie yelled back, "I'm coming. I just got out of the shower. I need coffee."

Natalie dressed and headed downstairs in her stocking feet. Rock and roll music blared and she slid into the kitchen in her socks, playing air guitar. Although one or two minor noises had startled her sleep in the night, she hadn't had any strange dreams.

Sunlight was streaming in the windows, some of which Mary had already opened. Around the mountains of boxes, the glossy hardwood reflected the light, making starbursts across the floor. Another beautiful morning in her new kingdom and all was well. So far, anyway.

Natalie looked out the back door. The landscaping fairies didn't make a visit in the middle of the night. The yard was still a nightmare.

Mary was rinsing her coffee cup in the sink. "Your phone is dead."

"I couldn't find the charger last night. It's got to be around here somewhere." She refilled her coffee and they both headed to the office down the hall. Neither mentioned the phone call about the house being haunted. It was too beautiful a day to talk about things going bump in the night.

She let out a heavy sigh when she saw all the boxes. At least the movers had put the heavy desk and bookshelves in the right places. She opened the drapes. It was a corner room so it had windows on two sides. She thought it was perfect for an office the first moment she saw it. The room was painted a light khaki color and she knew exactly which of her paintings would complement the walls. She was excited for her collection to arrive. Natalie had contracted a company that specialized in moving art and sculpture. She'd heard far too many horror stories about moving companies losing boxes. It was expensive, but worth it. She couldn't wait to set up her painting studio upstairs. She grabbed a dust rag sitting on the shelf, stuck another in her back pocket, clicked her box cutter, and got to work.

Natalie had her head in a box and her fanny in the air when she heard Mary come in with the phone installer. She bolted upright and hit her head on the desk, knocking herself flat to the floor.

"Damn it, that hurt." She felt dizzy and lay still for a moment.

"Are you all right?"

Natalie struggled to open her eyes. She saw an outline of a woman against the bright light from the windows. Brown hair hung in clouds around a face that she couldn't quite make out. A small hand brushed her forehead.

"Wha…" Natalie wiped her hands down her face and tried to focus. She tried again. "What? Who are you?"

"It's Sarah, silly. You must have hit your head hard." The woman tucked her legs under her dress and sat beside Natalie. "Poor baby. Do you need for me to kiss it?" She pulled Natalie's head into her lap to examine the bump.

Natalie let her eyelids drop for a second. The scent of lavender filled her nose. She felt a pull of longing at the sound of this woman's voice. *Who's Sarah?* She looked at the face above her. She felt some shock when she realized it was the woman from the painting. Big, soft brown eyes regarded her with concern, and Sarah leaned over and kissed her forehead. Silky strands of long hair fell around Natalie's face. She wanted to stay right here forever.

She stared at the stranger who seemed so familiar, and feeling tenderness toward the woman, hesitantly touched her face.

Sarah leaned in and kissed her. Natalie kissed her back, feeling as if she'd done it a thousand times before.

"Natalie?" A hand shook her shoulder hard.

"Natalie, wake up." The voice grew louder.

"Ow. Quit yelling at me." Natalie rubbed the back of her head. She looked around quickly and settled her gaze on Mary's face in front of her. "I don't suppose you saw her, did you?"

"Saw who, honey?" Mary looked worried. "Stay here. I'm going to go get some ice."

"Dude. That was cool." The phone tech sat back on his heels. "I heard your head crack all the way in the hall. Are you sure you're okay?"

Despite how odd she felt, Natalie smirked. "I'm just stellar, dude."

"Right," he said, drawing the word out into three syllables. Well, I'm going to finish installing your phone now. Can you move out of the way please?"

Natalie stood slowly and went into the living room. While sitting quietly in a chair, she tried to analyze what had happened and why she felt so sad. She reasoned it must be a hallucination as a result of hitting her head. That the woman in the painting was part of it clearly had to be a subconscious thing. The only thing not freaking her out at the moment was the kiss they shared. Natalie loved it. She would have to mull over that later. Mary came back in with some ice for her head. "Stay here," she ordered. "I'll take care of the phone guy."

Natalie wanted to call her back and tell her what she had seen, but stopped herself. She didn't feel she could explain it without sounding completely crazy. She could hear Mary in the office talking with the newly arrived cable technician. She traced the outline of her mouth with the tip of her fingers. The room was hot but she shivered against a sudden chill. She felt a soft fluttering on her cheek but didn't see an open window in the room. She swore there was a hint of lavender in the air and she felt a hand smooth her hair. Natalie shifted on the pillow. Now she *knew* she was going crazy. How was it possible for her to yearn for something she never had?

"Nat, honey? What's wrong?" Mary sat beside her and pulled Natalie's hand into hers. "Does it still hurt?"

Not trusting herself to speak with the lump in her throat, Natalie shook her head. She made a decision not to say anything to Mary just yet. She didn't think she could answer the questions that Mary would have. Instead, she dried her tears and stood. "C'mon, let's get something to drink."

"All finished in here." The phone guy popped his head in the doorway. "I left the invoice with your new phone number on the desk. If you have any problems, just give us a call."

Natalie showed him out. "Thank you." She closed the door and rested her head against it for a moment. She felt a warm breath on her neck and she looked back uneasily. A loud crash and scream came from the kitchen.

Natalie ran into the room. "What happened?" She took in the details of Mary's white face and the broken glass on the floor.

"I thought I saw something run across the room."

Natalie felt her stomach drop. "What kind of something?"

"It was nothing, just my imagination. Sorry about the glass."

Natalie carefully stepped over the ice and water. "S'okay, buddy. What's next on our list?"

Mary smoothed her shorts and started listing the work they had already completed. "Damn, we're good, lady. At this point, I think the art moving company is the only thing we're waiting for."

Natalie's fingers grew warm. They always did that when she thought of painting. Impatiently, she rubbed them against her legs. Like an addiction, the paints and canvases called to her. Mary washed her hands. "It's that time, Nat. I have to go and pick up the boys from school. Ready to face the monsters yet?"

Natalie hugged her. "Not tonight, I still have a headache. I'll eat some of that pasta salad you brought me and go to bed early."

"Are you sure you don't want to go and get that lump looked at? I don't like that you blacked out."

"I'm sure. Thank you."

Mary headed for the front door. "Call me if you need me, okay?" She blew Natalie a kiss on her way out.

Natalie made sure the front door was locked and stopped to look into her office. She leaned slightly and warily peeked over the top of her desk. She almost expected Sarah to be sitting on the floor. She felt her blood heat as she remembered the kiss. *What was that about?*

Chapter Five

Van drove up the long driveway leading to the old house, feeling a tingle on the back of her neck. She vaguely remembered her father telling her that one of her great-whatever-many-times-grandfather used be the head gardener for the original owners.

She had bragged about it when she was sixteen and her friends thought it would be fun to party in the abandoned house. So one stormy night, armed with beer, flashlights, and sleeping bags, they paired off and spread out throughout the rooms.

She couldn't help but grin when she also recalled that she made out with the head cheerleader, Missy, that night. If the other kids were scared and reported slamming doors and spooky knocking noises, she hadn't heard them over her raging hormones. Van didn't believe in ghosts. She had, however, believed in making it to second base with Missy Barnes.

The state of the grounds on either side of the driveway brought her back to the present. Karen Small had come to the nursery earlier in the week. While Van was ringing her purchase, Karen mentioned that the new owner of the old Seeley place might need the services of a good landscaper because she was certain it would be too much work for an individual to take on by herself. Karen pulled out a business card and wrote the new owner's name on the back of it.

Van continued to the house and mentally made an automatic checklist of what was needed to restore the gardens. Maybe the new owner would trust her experience to design a new plan for the yard. Oleander trees, azaleas, and rhododendrons grown out of control encroached on the driveway; thimbleberry and oxalis grew haphazardly around the scattered coastal trees; weeds and grass as tall as an adult in some areas, ran through the acreage. The sweet smell of honeysuckle in the sunny afternoon wafted through her open window and Van took a deep breath. She loved the amazing beauty of the California coast and knew she wouldn't want to live anywhere else.

The house came into view and she admired the wraparound porch. She didn't remember the house being pink before, but the color really stood out now. Definitely not a choice she would have made, but then again, she didn't own it.

By the time Van reached the door, she had already processed approximate cost, and how many of her crew she would need, though she wouldn't know for certain until she saw the back of the house. She pulled the owner's name out of her back pocket. The nursery did well, but she was excited about the scope of this job, and it would give her crew something to do during the summer. She reconsidered the size of the property and amended that estimate of time to continue right through the fall. They were booked solid for the next few weeks of spring.

Van heard the click of the dead bolt opening and had to look down at the woman who answered the door. She was momentarily caught off guard. Damn, she was a sucker for a redhead. Especially ones with freckles sprinkled across their nose and eyes as green as diamond cut emeralds. She cleared her throat and handed her one of her landscaping cards. So much for her standard business pitch. The woman stared back at her. It was the woman from the store parking lot, the one whose pockets she admired.

"Van Easton." She finally managed to blurt out before she stuck out her hand.

The woman shook her hand. "Hello."

Van cleared her throat again. "Mrs. Chambers?"

A split second of sadness passed over her face. "Nope, someone else has that title now. Natalie O'Donnell. What can I do for you?" Her smile was polite, pretty, and soft.

Van licked her lips, suddenly wishing she had some water. "Well, actually, Natalie, it's what I can do for you." She indicated the grounds with a sweep of her arm. "I ran into Karen a few days ago and she mentioned that you might need a landscaper."

Natalie twitched and looked around Van.

Van backed up a step on the porch. The seconds ticked by into a full minute. *What? Doesn't she know what her yard looks like?* "Ma'am?" Van saw a flicker of fear in her expression.

"I could certainly use some help," Natalie said. "The grounds weren't something I considered when I bought the place and it's going to need a major reconstruction."

Van relaxed a little. "Do you mind if I look around?"

"Let's start in the back." Natalie led her around the side of the house.

Van caught herself checking out the way Natalie's shorts shifted with her swaying walk, reminding her of the first time she saw her ass. She could smell her shampoo, fresh and citrusy, and it made her mouth water.

Little warning bells went off in her head and she went back to assessing the project. Hadn't she learned her lesson about straight women? Natalie herself said she was divorced. Why then, was her gaydar pinging? Must be wishful thinking on her part, she concluded. Besides, it was never a good idea to get involved with a client. She wanted this job.

❖

Van parked her truck, sat back, and closed her eyes. She wondered just how fast she could complete the estimate for the house on the hill. Van knew it wasn't just the job itself she was excited about. Thoughts of the attractive but skittish new client had teased her on the drive home. Natalie was certainly jumpy when she finished giving Van a tour of the grounds, her arms folded tightly across her chest as she constantly looked over her shoulder. She was even more nervous when they were at the back of the house and stood off to the side of the porch while Van took measurements and circled around with her clipboard. When she was done, she told Natalie she would write a proposal and get back with her soon.

Natalie seemed more at ease when they got back to the front of the house and the smile she gave Van was genuine, lighting her face and creating sunshine in the small space between them. She gave a hesitant wave when Van drove away.

Van got out of the truck and headed for the front door of her small house. Five years ago, it had been falling apart, crumbling slowly, but she had been able to see the good bones beneath the wilting exterior. She had bought it and with her father's help had restored it from the inside out. The front door opened before she could put her key in.

"Jesus. Candy, you scared the hell out me!" Over the workday, Van had forgotten about the woman she had brought home from the bar the night before, as well as the fact she had uncharacteristically told the woman she could hang out at her house. She made yet another promise to herself to quit drinking so much.

"I'm so sorry." Candy giggled and opened the door for her and stood to the side while she came in. Freshly showered and dressed only in one of Van's work shirts and skimpy white panties, she had obviously made herself at home. The living room was cleared of last night's revelry.

Candy stretched on her toes to kiss her, but Van turned her head and Candy's mouth brushed her cheek instead. "Is something wrong?"

Van hesitated then turned around. "Listen, Candy. I didn't expect you to still be here." She felt awkward and was reminded why she didn't like to have women stay over. She liked her, and this wasn't the first time they had fallen into bed together. It simply hit too close to a relationship for Van's comfort. She opened her mouth, but Candy cut her off before she could answer.

"Please don't use that bullshit line, it's-not-you-it's-me. Spare me the clichés, all right? Better yet, don't say anything." She threw her arms out for emphasis. "I'm leaving. I don't need this shit."

She left Van standing by the refrigerator, stunned. *Well, that certainly went well.*

A few minutes later, Candy slammed out of the bedroom completely dressed with her big purse bouncing off the side of the wall. "You know what really sucks, Van? I can't even say that you promised me anything." She wiped a tear off her cheek.

Even though she knew the crying to be ego rather than heartbreak, Van reached out a hand to her to stop her from running out the door. "Candy, please—"

"Please what, Van?" Candy put out a hand to block Van's. "Don't touch me right now. Just leave me my fucking dignity." She slammed the door on her way out.

Van stood looking at the closed door for a moment. *I'm sorry I can't be who you want me to be. I'm sorry I can't love you.*

Love had died six years ago. Van could still remember every single word that was spoken in that hospital room the day Cara died.

Cara lay in that uncomfortable bed, hooked up to God knows how many monitors, various tubes running in different directions. Her dark hair was matted with sweat and the purple circles under her eyes were prominent on her pale and gaunt face. She was still the most beautiful woman Van had ever seen.

Van sat in the chair next to the bed and held her hand, taking care not to bump the IVs. Her tears fell freely as she shook her head. "Don't talk like that. I don't want anyone but you. You're going to get better. You'll see."

Cara spoke softly but with intent. "I want you to love and be loved. Promise me, Vanessa. Promise me you will look for happiness."

Van couldn't breathe, grief punctured her heart, and she was so damn tired. She didn't want to say good-bye to the woman she had loved for the last decade. She sure as hell couldn't think about loving anyone else. So she lied. She looked Cara straight in the eye and promised her anything, anything at all, if it would help ease her suffering.

A tender smile spread across Cara's face and she let go. She took a long breath in, and did not take another.

It was a promise Van had yet to keep. When the darkness grew over the loneliness until it became more than she could bear, she headed out to drown the despair. There was always a willing soul who could see her pain and wanted to fix her, at least for a night anyway. She was halfway out the door to find one of those willing female souls when her emptiness warred with self-loathing, and suddenly, all she wanted to do was lounge on the couch and watch some television. Alone.

❖

"What's that stupid grin on your face for?" Van's father teased her.

"Got a new client."

"Oh?" her father asked. "Anyone I know?"

"Nope. It's a woman Karen Small told me about." Van put her elbows on the table and rested her chin on her hands. "Remember… the one who bought the Seeley place."

"Oh, yes, that's right. I heard about her when the boys were over for poker. Stan met her. Have you gone to see her already?"

Van nodded. "I went last week. We just made an appointment for tomorrow morning to go over the estimate."

"That was quick. I know we've been swamped with the spring rush. Did you tell her that someone in your family worked there a hundred years ago?"

"Yes, I did. Natalie loved the idea."

He grinned and winked at her. "Oh, I get it."

"You get what?"

"Stan told me she was a cute little redhead. Was he right?"

"Okay, you win. She's really short." Van held a hand to a point just below her shoulder. "She reminds me of the woman who played Agent Scully in the *X-Files*. She's divorced and really shy." Van squinted at her father. "Why are you asking me this anyway? She's just a client, Dad."

"Well, she is new in town and you got a funny look on your face when you said her name. Hey, weren't you going out with that little blonde, what's her name, Cindy?"

"I did not get a funny look. Her name was Candy, Dad. And no, we're not going out anymore."

"Seriously, Vannie. Are you ever going to settle down again?"

"Why the sudden interest?" Van leaned back. "You've never asked me that."

"Maybe I'm tired of seeing just your face at Sunday dinner. Maybe I want a pretty new face to smile at."

"Then maybe you should start dating, old man." She grinned so he knew she was kidding.

He refused to let it go. "It can't be healthy for you, all that drinking and running around that you do. Don't you miss having someone to come home to and talk with?"

Van leaned over the desk. "I had my shot, Dad. And she died. I was happy and I loved Cara with everything in me. I won't ever find that again, ever. I'm not sure I even want to." She left the office muttering under her breath. "I've got work to do."

Chapter Six

A beautiful fountain bubbled in the yard. It was a classic design with a cherub pouring water out of a jug. The only thing different about it was the unusual size. It was large enough Natalie could feel the water spray from where she was standing, five feet away. Rainbows sparkled in the mist where the sun was shining through the crystal droplets of water. She looked around in astonishment. Carefully trimmed rosebushes of red, yellow, pink, and white lined the walkway into the garden on the side of the house. Dark purple blooms from a giant lilac framed the arbor. Purple pansies burst out of planters. Red geraniums battled with yellow in more containers. It was gorgeous.

Natalie sat on a pretty stone bench nestled amongst bleeding fuchsias to the side of the fountain and for the first time noticed the blue summer dress she was wearing. The only times she ever wore dresses were at her gallery showings. As a matter of fact, the only one she'd brought with her was a little black number, one of the few her ex-husband hadn't picked out for her.

"There you are. I've been looking everywhere for you."

Natalie turned sharply, her pulse leaping.

Sarah stood framed in the afternoon sunshine in a yellow dress. Her dark hair was loose under a matching wide-brimmed hat. Natalie could see a fine line of sweat on her upper lip. On her arm was a basket filled with recently cut flowers and she held clippers in her gloved hand.

"Hello," she said softly then sat next to Natalie. "You'll get sunstroke out here without your hat. If we wait awhile, we can go to the beach as soon as it cools off a little." She fanned her face.

Natalie cleared her throat, but no sound would come out. She knew she was staring at Sarah's mouth, but she couldn't seem to stop herself. She felt her face turning red and knew it wasn't from the sun. Tentatively, she reached out and touched Sarah's shoulder.

"Look at me, dear heart. You're trembling. What's the matter?"

Natalie managed to shake her head and whispered, "You are so beautiful. I don't understand any of this. I think I must be losing my mind."

"And why would you think that, love?" She brought Natalie's hand to her mouth. Very gently, she kissed and nibbled the tip of her index finger.

Natalie felt as if a sledgehammer hit her. Her stomach twisted, and she shivered slightly before looking into Sarah's eyes, seeing only desire reflected back to her.

"I know what you need. Come along. It's too hot, don't you think? We should be lying down in the heat of the day." Her voice dropped to a whisper. "I'll come to you as soon as the housekeeper leaves to go shopping. Be waiting for me." Sarah disappeared back into the side garden.

Natalie nervously tucked a strand of hair behind her ear. She decided it was stupid to be nervous because this had to be a dream, right? She raced up to her room and stepped out of her pretty dress. Natalie stood in front of the cool ocean breeze coming in the window for a moment before she lay on the bed in her slip. It *was* hot and she positively ached with desire. What was taking Sarah so long?

When she woke to a noise some time later, it was dark and Natalie realized she must have been moaning out loud. Her hips were undulating against the hand she'd tucked between her legs sometime during the night. She was so disappointed she didn't get to finish the dream about Sarah. Natalie held the image of her face and the look in Sarah's eyes while she continued to rock against her hand; maybe *this* time she could have an orgasm. It had been so long since she'd tried. She closed her eyes, reveling in the pounding sensation between her thighs.

Hot female skin slid over her naked body, soft curves fit against her own. Natalie shivered and arched her back. Natalie was lost in her fantasy but couldn't help but remember all those years she wasted, thinking something was wrong with her. That she wasn't capable of this passion or response. She opened her legs to give Sarah room to kneel between them.

Shouts filtered in the open window from outside. The voices were male.

Sarah rose in a panic. "I need to go. He can't find us like this." She grabbed a robe from the end of the bed and ran out of the room.

"Who can't find us here like this?" Natalie said to the empty room. The front door slammed so hard, she jumped and frantically looked for a place to hide. Heavy footsteps thudded on the stairs. One after the other, growing louder with each step until the bedroom door flew open and hit the wall.

A very large, very angry man stood in the doorway dressed in black. His shoulders filled the doorframe and rage distorted his face. He took a step into the room and slammed the door shut.

❖

Natalie's eyes snapped open, her breath coming in gasps. She was almost paralyzed with fear, and damp with cold sweat, she stared into the dark. The man wasn't in her room and nothing assaulted her. After a few moments, she snapped the lamp switch on her nightstand. The window was open and the air in her room was cold. She rubbed her arms briskly in an attempt to warm them. What the hell just happened?

A quick look and she saw she was still dressed in the same rumpled tank and shorts she'd gone to bed in. She knew the encounter with Sarah was just a dream, but Natalie's very real physical reaction was still lingering. She made an effort to control her breathing so she could slow her heart rate down and try to think. She'd just had the most amazing sexual experience in her life and it was a fricking dream? But why did she feel as if it were so real? She had a vivid flash of velvet skin against hers, breast to breast and thigh to thigh; long, silky hair wrapping her in lavender fragrant softness.

After she calmed a little, she went into the bathroom where she splashed cold water on her face and looked into the mirror. What she saw made her pulse quicken all over again. She blinked then touched her changed reflection in the mirror. Her lips were swollen and her neck showed little red marks. She felt her stomach tighten and gripped the counter for support.

She felt a little sad. Could it be that she was manifesting these dreams because of the divorce? Was she reacting to her upheaval and sense of rejection by creating an imaginary lover who really desired her? Why did she feel that she knew Sarah, and who the hell was that man in black?

❖

The next morning, Natalie sat on the front porch swing with her coffee and rocked back and forth, swinging her feet in rhythm. Last night's dream would not leave her alone. Her thoughts played like a DVD in slow frame. Images of soft female skin, sliding over her own would snap to the fear she felt when she saw the man in her doorway. She'd lain in bed until dawn, trying to put the sound of heavy footsteps in the hallway toward her hundred year old house. She had to; logically, she knew there was no one else in the house with her. She preferred not to think of the alternative. At least not until her mother arrived.

It wasn't until she heard a truck door slam that she noticed Van's white landscaping truck. Their appointment had slipped her mind.

Natalie watched her approach through the morning heat to the porch. Van's long, long legs wore faded 501s and she had on a white tank top with the words V & V Landscapers embroidered over her left breast. *Small, perfect breasts with hard nipples that I want to bite.*

The thought shocked her. Natalie felt her face flush and looked at the wooden planks. It didn't matter; the sight of Van was burned into her retinas. The next things she saw were Van's boots.

"Drop something?" Van slid her aviator sunglasses down her nose to peer at her and dropped her considerable height to a crouch.

"No." Natalie felt almost giddy. She looked into Van's ice-blue eyes and smiled. She wanted to reach and move the lock of platinum bangs to the side and stare longer. She wanted to run her tongue along her long neck and nibble on her ear. What was *wrong* with her? Natalie made a concentrated effort to pull herself together.

"Good morning." Van set the briefcase on the swing next to Natalie. "I've brought your estimates."

"Let's take them in the kitchen."

Natalie could feel Van's attention. She felt as if her skin was humming with an electrical charge and she asked herself why. She had met beautiful butch women before; she was an artist for God's sake, and from San Francisco, no less. Half the people she knew were gay. She didn't know if this attraction was real or a holdover from her erotic dream. She turned around, ridiculously pleased at the sound of a wolf whistle coming from behind her. Unfortunately, the appreciation was for the counters.

"Wow. There must be an acre of granite in here."

"I know, right? They did a wonderful job in here." Maybe she could ask Van some questions. "Did you ever meet them, the previous owners?

"No. From what I hear, they weren't here very long."

They stopped at the kitchen table, and Van set her paperwork on the table while Natalie poured a cup of coffee.

"Would you like some?" Natalie gestured toward the pot.

"No, thanks."

"Do you know any of the stories about the house?"

"Only that my ancestor worked here. I could ask my father about the stories."

"Could you? I would appreciate it." Natalie was a little relieved that Van didn't pop out with a gory story. She didn't think she could handle one today.

"Here are the costs and a blueprint for what I think would be the best layout for your property. We can change anything you want to or implement any ideas that you may have."

Natalie sat and tried to focus on the estimate. The plans looked wonderful and well thought out. The gardens would be restored where they should be and she liked the idea of having the grounds look the way they might have at the turn of the previous century. She noted the small tremor in the page she was holding and set it back down. The air seemed to thicken in the room and Natalie found it difficult to take a full breath. Her body pulsed with pent up desire, and *damn it*, she couldn't think with Van in the room and so close to her.

From the moment she'd stepped onto the porch, Van was aware of the sexual energy that sprang up between them. She couldn't quite pinpoint what was different, but the last time she'd been here to see Natalie, she was a nervous wreck. Now she seemed to be undressing her with her eyes. She was happy to return the favor and let her gaze travel. She liked everything about her but tried to pull it back to the business at hand.

Natalie said something she missed. Van tore her attention away from Natalie's chest to her face. "Excuse me?" Van was aware of the effect she had on women but rarely had she seen such blatant *need* in someone's expression. A strange emotion rose in her. She wanted to throw Natalie to the floor; she wanted her underneath her so she could *take her.* Possess her completely until she submitted and whimpered her pleasure. Where the hell had that come from? *Whoa, Vannie. Client here.*

"I just remembered." Natalie said abruptly. "I have another appointment. Could you come back later when I have time to go over the new designs with you? Or perhaps I could come to the nursery if that would be more convenient for you?" Natalie's pen moved with lightning speed as she signed the estimate.

"Aren't you going to read them?"

"I trust you."

Van was a little surprised at the dismissal and still reeling from her fantasy. "Of course. Either way, just call me when you have the time. We could try and have the first cleanup crew here in a couple of weeks or so. At least on half days with our schedule so booked."

Van followed her down the hall. She grinned when she passed the closet under the arched stairs, remembering the last time she'd been in the house. But there was no way she was going to tell her new client about the foray into her closet so many years ago. She had the oddest sensation of feeling watched. She glanced behind her, but there was no one there.

She sat in her truck for a moment, staring through her windshield at the house. The drapes in one of the front windows on the second floor moved and she wondered if Natalie was watching her leave. This had to be one of the fastest and strangest meetings she'd ever had with a client.

Chapter Seven

"Okay then," Natalie said to the closed door after Van left. She almost felt like crying, but whether that was because she wanted Van to stay, or because she felt as though her life was caught in a Stephen King novel, she didn't know.

She turned to leave but heard tires crunching on the driveway and quickly opened the door. She was excited to think that maybe Van had forgotten something and come back. Why would she? Natalie had practically thrown her out after signing the estimate.

A strange car pulled in behind her Mercedes. Natalie let out an excited squeal when she saw her mother get out and ran off the porch to greet her before she had even shut the car door.

Her mother held Natalie at arm's length. "Hi, baby. Let me look at you."

"Mom, I'm so glad you're here. Did you have any problems? What do you think?" Natalie rattled off the questions rapidly, not pausing long enough for an answer.

"Slow down, sweetheart. I just got here. Let's go inside. My bag is in the backseat. Could you get it for me?"

Natalie grabbed the bag and ran ahead of her so she could enter the house first. "My mother is here," she shouted through the doorway. She grabbed her mother's hand and they entered into the foyer. They weren't in the door four steps before the front door slammed behind them.

"How cheesy is that?" Natalie asked.

"He's making a statement, I suppose."

"*He*?" Natalie said, thinking of the man in her nightmare.

Her mother spotted the painting and headed straight for it. A contemplative look crossed her face as she studied it. She reached out to touch it and drew back as if she'd been burned.

"I *knew* it had something to do with this painting. She looks so familiar to me, Mom. I could swear it's been doing some Dorian Gray thing on me." Natalie chose not to tell her mother of the erotic dreams, yet. At some point she knew she would discuss it. Maybe.

"It's a doorway," her mother said.

"Crap. I was hoping you were going to tell me I'm suffering from an overactive imagination." Natalie pushed her hand through her hair and started pacing back and forth in front of the painting.

Her Mother smiled then hesitated slightly. "The woman in the painting, she's not the only one here."

"Would that be the 'he' you were referring to?" Natalie shivered and looked over her shoulder.

"Yes. Let's get the normal stuff out of the way, shall we? I've had a long flight and drive. I'm just not ready for kicking some spirit fanny just yet. Okay?"

"Of course. I'm sorry." Natalie hoisted her mother's bag and headed for the stairs. "It's just that things have been so weird this last week. Things are happening that make no sense and I've been a little spooked. Let me show you to the guest room. It even has its own bathroom."

"Your new house is lovely, Natalie. I'm looking forward to seeing the rest of it."

❖

With her mother safely upstairs napping, Natalie sat on the couch in the living room, curling her legs to the side. She debated calling Mary, but with last night's dream several hours behind her, she didn't feel the same urgency that she did this morning. She was reluctant to bother her since she had done so much for her in the last month. She looked over at the painting. Sarah hadn't moved again. Natalie had almost convinced herself that she perceived the painting incorrectly the first night she was here. Now, after what her mother told her, she knew that wasn't the case. Her thoughts drifted to the beautiful woman smiling shyly at her. That was some fantasy. She could not stop thinking about how incredibly turned on she was by the whole dream. Well, until the end of it, anyway. In all her life, she had never thought of women that way until she moved into this house. *Liar.*

A thick black wall of denial crumbled. A myriad of images and feelings swirled in her mind. Her artwork rushed to the front of her mind. Her paintings were always of women. There was Cleopatra, stretching like a cat on her chaise couch, sultry, yet aloof. Lady Godiva, naked and fiercely glorious on her horse. Helen of Troy, on the balcony watching a thousand ships in the distance. Each one of the women portrayed as strong and seemingly untouchable by mere mortals. Natalie felt truly alive when she was painting.

Why did she paint only women? Why not the elusive Prince Charming on his unattainable white horse? The answer was so obvious: she loved everything about women. The graceful curve of a neck, the slope of a shoulder, and the curve of a waist giving way to round hips.

Scores of Goddesses were held locked in her imagination until she made them real on canvas. Natalie recalled the passion that consumed her when she was painting. The women belonged to her and she knew that she made love to them with every stroke of her paintbrush.

Small guilty teeth nipped at her conscious. In doing what was thought was expected from her when she married, it appeared she had completely denied who she was.

Natalie put her hands over her face and groaned. A couple of years ago, for her nude *Angel in Paradise* painting, she'd hired a new model. Natalie had been mesmerized by the long, silky hair that rained down the woman's back. As Natalie posed her, she remembered sliding her hand along the sides of the girl's luscious breasts, caressing her waist and lightly touching her buttocks to position her the way she wanted her, just so. She tried to tell herself it was the artist in her, but if she wanted to be consistent at being completely honest, and it seemed at this point that she must, she felt that girl up.

Oh God, I'm a letch too.

❖

"Nat? Your paintings are here." Her mother called her from the foyer.

"Finally! I've felt naked without them." Natalie tried to hide the fact she'd been crying by keeping her face turned away. "There's fresh coffee in the kitchen if you want some. I'll just go out and meet them."

"Okay. Then we'll talk about why you are so upset and why you've been crying."

Busted. "How do you do that?" Natalie spun from the door to look at her mother.

"Natalie, I've read your mind your whole life. Why are you still surprised?"

"I keep thinking it's going to wear off with age or something," Natalie answered under her breath.

She let the movers in and directed them to the turret room where her paintings would be stored. She blatantly ignored the supervisor, Josh, an overweight, sweaty, rude man who didn't even try to hide the leer on his face while he checked her out. She watched them for a moment to make sure they were showing proper reverence to her paintings then left them to it.

She found her mother in the kitchen looking out the window over the sink with her head cocked to the side as if she were studying something. "Did you see something unusual out here?"

"That's one of the first strange things that happened to me here, Mom. I was standing where you were, and when I looked outside, the garden was immaculate. It looked like a photo straight out of a *Better Homes and Garden* spread. When I rushed outside, I realized it was an illusion. Scared the bejesus out of me. I thought it was stress or something."

"I can sense a strong energy outside the window."

"An entity?"

"No. Residual. More like a recording. Something important happened out there. The strong emotion tied to the area is looping around and around, playing itself out, and then repeating."

Natalie tapped her fingernail on the table. "How come I've never experienced this phenomenon before?"

"I don't know, Nat. I've always sensed a psychic spark in you, but you never brought it up or asked me any questions, so maybe you just blocked it. Or maybe it's just something to do with *this* house and *these* ghosts."

Natalie thought of everything else she had blocked in her life, including herself. She opened her mouth, but before she could speak, a crash and yell sounded from the stairs and brought them to their feet. Natalie was the first one out the kitchen door. She found Josh at the bottom of the second floor landing swearing and holding his ankle. His face was angry and red. "Who the hell pushed me?"

Natalie looked behind him. "There doesn't seem to be anyone else there. Are you all right? Do you want me to call an ambulance or something?"

Josh twisted his neck to look up the stairs. "I could have sworn someone was behind me. I thought it was one of my guys." His voice trailed off when his two laborers entered the front door with another load. "Really."

Colleen clucked over him. "It might have been a loose floorboard, dear. Maybe you were going too fast and missed a step," she said sweetly. "Would you like me to get some ice for that?"

Natalie bit back a giggle. She was just talking with her mother about spirit doorways, ghosts, and psychic energy in the house, and she was blaming the man's own clumsiness? God, she loved her.

Josh looked more embarrassed than hurt. "No, thanks. This here is the last load. Ms. Chambers, I have your inventory list." There was no sign of his leering at her now. "Could you please check this stuff off?"

As soon as Natalie reached the top of the stairs, the air seemed to rustle around her. It was faint, but she could definitely hear a trace of laughter. She looked down the hall.

"Sarah, did you push that nasty man?" She stood there for a few moments, but she didn't see or hear anything else. Maybe her haunting could have its fun moments. It certainly seemed to be protective.

Natalie looked out the floor-length windows in the turret. She was once again struck by how much she loved this room and the endless view of the ocean. Natalie pulled out her copy of the inventory list. She spread it out on the corner desk to compare the two. Everything was numbered and so organized it only took a few minutes to ascertain that all her paintings were there and in good condition. She was filled with anticipation bordering on Christmas morning excitement. She couldn't wait to start painting. She carefully closed the door at the bottom of the stairs to keep the cool air in place and joined her mother in the living room, who was entertaining the work crew with her tarot cards.

Josh took the finished checklist from her hand and limped toward the door. "We appreciate your business. I'm off to make my fortune and meet the woman of my dreams according to the cards and your mother. Let's go, guys."

After they left, Natalie looked at her mother, amused. "The cards didn't really say that, did they?"

"No, but I had fun."

"Mother." Natalie laughed.

Chapter Eight

Natalie wondered if she would ever tire of watching the sunshine bounce off the ocean, but it was so bright she was glad she was wearing her Ray-Bans. "This is so charming. I love it!"

"I haven't been able to come very often, but now that you've moved here, I hope to come here more frequently. It's hard to interest the boys in a farmers market," Mary said, testing a tomato.

"Did you call each other this morning to see what the other was wearing?" Natalie's mother caught up to them on the boardwalk. "You look like the Bobbsey twins." She straightened her colorful gypsy broom skirt and adjusted the wide-brimmed straw hat on her head.

Mary smiled and motioned at the crowd in front of them. "It's Bayside's uniform, see?"

They all laughed when they caught sight of at least a third of the crowd wearing cutoff jeans and sleeveless blouses. The only difference in some was in the name brands. Some people paid more for casual.

"Nat? Are we looking for anything in particular or are we just browsing?" Her mother pointed to the left side of the market. "I want to check out the candles and that interesting looking crystal booth over there. Either come find me or I'll find you. The place isn't that big."

Natalie watched her leave, her colorful clothes blowing behind her. "God, I love my mother."

"Who wouldn't? She's a wonderful character. How long is she staying?"

"Dad called last night, says he's falling apart without her. So I'm not sure."

"Is he really?"

"No. My father's perfectly able to take care of himself. He just misses her something fierce when she's away. He gets bored."

"I can see how life with your mother could be far from boring."

"Mmmm." Natalie's attention was drawn to a large section in the far corner. She could see various yard sculptures, colorful plants and benches, and hear the sound of wind chimes in the slight breeze. She felt herself drawn to the display.

When she got closer, she could also hear splashing water. The sound hitched in her stomach, reminding her of the dream of Sarah and the fountain.

"Can I help you?"

Natalie let her eyes follow the sound of the voice. "Um…" Natalie felt a sexual tug when Van approached her. She tried clearing her throat. "Um…" She felt stupidly tongue-tied.

Mary came to her rescue. "Hi, my friend just moved here and I was showing her around. Is this a new business? I don't recall seeing it here before." She held her hand out to her. "I'm Mary, and this is my friend Natalie."

"I'm Van. It's nice to meet you, Mary. Natalie and I have met, and yes, this is my first year here at Bayside Farmers Market. I started a landscaping design business out of my father's nursery not too long ago. This is my attempt to snare business for the rest of the year." Van took a step closer to Natalie and took her hand. "How are you?"

Natalie wanted to sigh but smiled instead. At least, she hoped it was a winning smile; her face felt a little numb. Mary interrupted. "Can we look around? You have some beautiful art here."

Van let go of Natalie's hand slowly and smiled. "Of course. Yell if you need something."

Natalie let Mary lead her over to the fountain structure. She could feel an itch between her shoulder blades. Sure enough, when she glanced back, Van's eyes were glued to her. She flushed with an unfamiliar heat between her thighs. She tried to concentrate on what Mary was saying. She nodded at what she hoped were appropriate places, but her gaze kept tracking back to where Van was standing.

"Hey!" Mary slapped Natalie's bare arm. "You haven't heard a word I've said."

"Ouch. I have too, smarty."

"What was I talking about?" Mary stuck a hand on her hip.

"Um…you know…about…stuff!"

"Stuff?" Mary chuckled and then narrowed her eyes in mock annoyance. "You have no clue, do you?"

Natalie gave up the pretense and shrugged. "Not a one. Have you looked at her?" She fanned her face with her hand. "No, don't look. She's watching."

"Who are you talking about?" Mary turned around in confusion. "She who?"

Natalie shot her a look and then panicked. "Oh God, don't look now. Here she comes. What do I do?"

Van stopped when she stood next to Natalie and whispered in her ear, "Do you like what you see?" she asked.

Natalie sputtered. Had Van read her mind? "Excuse me? What did you say?"

"The fountain. Do you like the fountain?"

"Oh, you mean the *fountain*! Yes, I love it." Natalie was mortified at what she had been thinking; she tried to play it off. "Did you design it?"

"I did."

"Oh? How interesting." *Great, Natalie, you dumbass. Think of something to say.*

Natalie turned to Mary, silently imploring her to say something.

"Aren't you guys located off Highway Three? I've never been there, though I've heard it's lovely," Mary jumped in.

Van smiled politely. "Thank you. Natalie, could I talk to you for a minute?" She drew her out a couple of feet away.

Natalie felt a little lightheaded. “Yes?” Had she even managed more than two-syllable words since she met this woman?

“Will you go out to dinner with me tonight?”

“No.” Natalie flushed and stuttered when she saw the disappointed look on Van’s face.

“No. I mean, I can’t go tonight. I can the next night, though.”

“Okay, then.” Her smile lit her eyes, and Natalie felt her knees turn to Jell-O.

“There you two are!” Natalie’s mother came running up, shopping bags swinging on her arms. “I need help with some of the other things I’ve bought.”

Mary took two bags from her. “Colleen, this is Van. Van, this is Natalie’s mother, Colleen.”

“Nice to meet you, Colleen.”

“You too.” Natalie’s mother looked at her, then Van and back again. “Uh, oh.”

Natalie waited until her mother and Mary were seated in the living room sipping a glass of wine before she decided she would get this conversation out of the way. She had successfully evaded their questions about Van and wanted to put her thoughts in order first. Her dreams and house were haunted by the lovely Sarah, and she’d finally broken through the wall of denial she’d been living behind for most of her life.

She was in the process of mentally preparing her speech, the bombshell she was about to drop when she felt her mother’s eyes swing over to her. Natalie paused for a minute and jumped in. “I have something to tell you.”

They both looked at her. “Okay, shoot.”

“I think I’m a lesbian.”

Mary paused for a second and took a sip of her drink. Her mother continued to look at her directly. Neither said anything.

“Did you hear what I just said?” Natalie raised her voice a little. “I said I’m a lesbian.”

Silence.

"Mom? Mary? Say something."

"Oh, honey," said her mother. "It took you long enough."

Mary sipped her wine. "I've often wondered. But what brought this on? Is this because of what Jason did to you?"

"What do you mean it took me long enough?" Natalie asked crossly. "I didn't even think about it until recently. You've often wondered? Why didn't anybody tell *me*?"

"Well, as much as I love you, Nat, I'm not leaving my husband."

Natalie spun around. "*What*?"

"She's only kidding, sweetheart. Now tell us, dear, how you came to this epiphany."

"God, I'm embarrassed at how cliché this all sounds. But, here goes. I never thought about boys at all while I was in school. I just never could see what the whole fuss was about. I just accepted the fact that I was the class geek and concentrated on my grades. It's not as if anyone wanted to date me anyway."

"You were adorable, Natalie." Her mother jumped to her defense.

"Mom. I had acne and braces. I stayed in my room all the time."

"But you outgrew all that," Mary said.

"Yes, I did, later. By the time I was finishing college I had still put everything I had into my studies and then painting. I just thought I was a late bloomer."

Her mother's tone was gentle. "Honey, do you remember when you used to watch *Lost in Space* reruns when you were growing up? What was that girl's name again? The middle one, you know, cute, long, dark hair."

Natalie smiled. "Penny. Her name was Penny."

"Yes, that's right. Penny. Do you remember telling me that you were going to marry her?"

"Mom, I was nine."

"Okay, do you remember the *Partridge Family*? The oldest sister, Laurie? I seem to recall you saying you had a crush on her also."

Natalie knew her face turned bright red. "Mom!"

"Oh, and let's not forget how you would never miss an episode of *Days of Our Lives,* with that Hope character, and—"

"Oh, I've got one!" Mary shot her hand in the air. "Pick me, pick me!"

Natalie's mother pointed obligingly. "Your turn, dear. Go ahead."

"Nat, do you remember all the hair bands? You loved them."

"Mary, they were men."

"No, Natalie. They were pretty, pretty boys with lots of hair and they wore makeup." She stirred in her chair. "Come to think of it, I loved them, also. Hmm. No, I'm just kidding. Nat, honey, all I have to do is look at your art and know how much you love women and their bodies. It completely personifies how beautiful women are." Mary smiled. "Would any of this have something to do with the blond Amazon today?"

Natalie looked at her folded hands. "Maybe, but I don't know if I would have considered dating her if it hadn't been for the dreams about Sarah."

"Is this Sarah the one in the painting?" her mother asked.

"I'm sure of it. I just have this feeling I know her. I mean, I thought she looked familiar before I had the dream, too. What did you mean, Mom, when you said this is a doorway?"

"Well, you telling me of your dream is proof of that theory. It is a feminine energy that comes through there. I also sense deep love and passion."

"Do you believe me that she's moved positions in the painting?"

"Wait a minute," Mary jumped in. "You didn't tell me about that. So you're telling me that woman *moved* in the painting then came on to you? Do you realize how that sounds?"

"Of course I realize how it sounds," Natalie snapped. "That's why I didn't tell you. Mom, do you think I'm going crazy?"

"No, Natalie. I don't think you're going crazy. I believe there are other forces at work here. We will try and research to get to the bottom of it. What do you know of the male spirit? Did you dream of him also?"

The hair on Natalie's arms stood on end. "He seems violent and I'm a little scared of him. But I don't know if it's *my* fear or Sarah's."

A look of disgust covered Mary's face. "*What* man spirit? *Now* what are you talking about?" She stopped, opened her mouth, and stopped again. "Oh. This has to do with the previous owners, right? And why everyone who has lived here in the past leaves."

"I think it's time you told us about what you've heard about this house. We can talk about my sexual orientation later." Natalie rolled her shoulders at the sudden tension in the room. "Is it me or is it colder in here?"

"The subject should be brought up in another location. If it's as negative as I think it is, the energy feeds off of attention. Especially fear."

"Can he hurt Natalie?" Mary asked.

"I'd love to say no, but I'm not sure. I don't know enough about it yet."

"But you will, I have faith in you. Now what do we do?"

"Now, we all go out for a nice dinner. Mary, can your men fend for themselves?"

"Why, yes, Miss Colleen. They certainly can. Let me just give them a quick call. I don't want to miss any of this. There's a great little restaurant on Main. We can go there."

"I'll grab a light sweater."

Natalie's mother stood and grabbed her purse. "Which one of you girls is paying?"

"I believe your daughter, the successful lesbian artist, can afford it," Mary said. "Oh, and don't think you're going to get out of telling us about that gorgeous woman at the market today, either."

Natalie was the last one out when she thought she heard a door slam upstairs. She quickly locked the door then ran to the car.

❖

Van was exhausted, but she had appointments for the next week with several potential new clients and her father would be happy. Breaking down the booth at the market was hard, tedious work, and she was hungry. She headed into the kitchen to see what she could make with a minimum of fuss. The beer bottles on the top shelf caught her eye and she snagged one out of habit and set it on the counter while she made a sandwich.

While she ate, Van checked her messages. One was from Annette, her team captain calling to remind her of their last softball game of the season tomorrow morning. The other was also from Annette, inviting her to come to Miss Apple's Tavern with the rest of the girls and play, although not necessarily a team sport.

Normally, Van would have wolfed the rest of her food and met them to avoid the loneliness that was a Saturday night staple for her. But tonight, just the thought of the whole bar scene tired her even more. Sitting at the table, staring at the bottle in front of her, Van stopped her hand in mid grab. Did she really want to get buzzed here by herself? Hadn't she done enough of that?

Condensation ran down the cold bottle to form a ring at its base. Van's mouth didn't water at the sight; instead she was reminded of falling tears. What was she doing with her life?

Natalie's face intruded into her thoughts. Weird, she hadn't thought much about how numb she had been until she met her. Numb was normal until she stepped her work boots onto Natalie's front porch. Van hadn't been a saint about female companionship since Cara died; she just wasn't really present. Not much made it past the ice fortress she had built around her heart. It hadn't mattered.

What had she been thinking asking a client out? The invitation was out of her mouth before she thought twice about it. She was so darn cute standing there looking at her with those big eyes. She looked innocent and sexy at the same time. It was turning out to be an intoxicating combination.

She felt a little sneaky, but she Googled Natalie Chambers anyway. Several links were listed on the home page, and the first one she clicked on was a Bay Area society article that mentioned her divorce. Another click and she came across a picture of Natalie in a little black dress standing next to a tall blond man with a toothy smile. Both were toasting something with their champagne glasses.

Van superimposed the image on the screen with Natalie this afternoon in cutoffs and tank top and decided she liked her casual much better. She spent the better part of an hour looking at thumbnails of Natalie's paintings. They were gorgeous. She didn't know much about art, but she would have known that these were painted by a woman. The nudity was soft and beautiful, hinting at sensuality.

Her favorite painting was the one of a red-haired goddess that appeared to be merged into the mountains and sunset behind her. She had no problem picturing Natalie's face in the painting, or Natalie on her back in her bed. Natalie's hair laying tangled on her pillows with a fine sheen of sweat on her naked skin. Van clenched her thighs together and imagined how she would touch, taste, and explore.

Jesus. When had her libido turned sixteen again? Van poured the beer down the sink and headed for a cold shower.

Chapter Nine

Natalie listened to her mother and Mary chatter in the front seat while on their way to the restaurant. She couldn't seem to concentrate. Her mind was reeling with questions and possibilities, but none of her thoughts seemed to run in any kind of sequence. She was confused and tired. She waited until they ordered and drinks were on the table before jumping into the conversation. "Okay, Mom. Can you tell more of what is going on in the house now?"

"First impression?"

"Yes."

"When I first arrived, on my way up to the house, I felt a barrier of sorts."

"Barrier? What kind?" asked Mary.

"It's a wall of energy that gives me a physical reaction. Cold chills, the hair rising on the back of my neck, things of that sort. Before I could get a handle on it, Natalie came barreling out of the house and it disappeared."

"And the painting?" asked Natalie. "You've said a couple of times that it was a doorway."

"Of sorts," her mother answered. "There's a strong feminine energy attached to it. I get the impression of powerful emotions. Love, passion, heartbreak, waiting."

"Waiting?"

Her mother paused. "It's hard to explain." She directed her attention to Mary's question. "It's that I can feel Sarah's emotions when I'm near it. My grandmother always explained it as the *Knowing*. There are times when there is a strong emotional attachment to an object, that spirit attaches itself to it. You hear of haunted objects in antique stores and such."

"That's residual emotions, right?"

"Right, but…"

"Go ahead, Mom. I'm a big girl."

"The longer I'm in the house, the energy doesn't feel residual. It feels trapped instead."

"Is this where the dark man comes in?" Mary asked.

"Yes. What I pick up from that energy is stronger. I've got the impression that he keeps Sarah trapped and she's unable to move on. He feeds off negative emotion and gets stronger."

"So it makes sense that he's the one I hear walking the hallways and slamming doors."

"What does all this have to do with Natalie?"

"I don't know all the answers, Mary. *Knowing* isn't an exact science; it's feelings and intuition."

Natalie felt a little helpless. "So what do we do about it?"

"We try and find out what we can about the history of the house and contact some of the previous owners to ask them what they experienced and why they left. We try and cleanse the house of the dark energy."

"What if it doesn't work?" asked Natalie.

"We'll cross that bridge when we come to it."

❖

Natalie stood in the hallway. She could hear voices that appeared to be having a conversation, but she couldn't quite make out what they were saying. She strained her ears to decipher the direction she should go.

The turret room.

She approached the door then watched her hand reach for the knob in slow motion. Natalie turned it quietly. What? Did she think she was going to sneak up on them in the dark? She felt as if she were swimming in ice water and her pulse beat loudly in her ears.

Natalie grabbed the banister for support. When she reached the top landing she hit the light switch. The room was empty, but the voices grew in volume, spinning around her, almost tangible like a speeding train. It was making her dizzy. Natalie put her hands over her ears and slid down the wall to sit on the floor with her knees drawn up to her chest.

The room stopped turning and Natalie lowered her hands.

"Stop fidgeting. You're ruining my lines."

Natalie's eyes snapped open and she saw Sarah standing by the window.

"It's too hot in here, Beth." Sarah fanned a hand in front of her face. "Can't we finish this later?"

"I'm almost done. Please, just a few more minutes? Go back to where you were. I want this to be perfect. Like you."

Natalie was puzzled by the additional voice. Who was Beth? She tried to see over the top of the easel but couldn't from her position on the floor. She felt frozen in place.

"You think I'm perfect?" Sarah's cheeks turned pink.

"Yes. Now please, get back into position."

Natalie was amused at Beth's tone of voice. She herself had used it on many occasions when painting a live model.

Sarah turned toward the window and placed one hand on the frame, the other along the back of the armchair beside her.

The second Natalie saw her flip her long hair behind her she immediately recognized the pose in the oil painting downstairs. A low electrical charge seemed to buzz along her skin. She was more curious than afraid but gasped anyway when Beth moved out from behind the easel. She looked like Natalie's twin, right down to the mole she had to the left of her upper lip. She was a much younger version and her hair was longer, but the resemblance was so strong it was spooky. Suddenly, the dreams of making love with Sarah made more sense. It wasn't Natalie that Sarah saw. It was this look-alike,

Beth. Natalie was completely enthralled with the scene in front of her.

Sarah jumped when Beth approached from behind and lightly grazed the tips of her breasts through the thin material.

"You're nipples were hard when we started," Beth said then kissed the side of Sarah's long neck. "Now don't move. Hold it just like that."

Beth crossed back to the easel and hours seemed to pass in seconds while Natalie watched her mix paint and the brushes fly to the canvas. In her mind's eye, she painted along with her.

"Are you finished yet?"

"Yes."

"Can I see?"

Beth put down her brushes. A blue smear crossed her cheek and her hands were covered in paint splatter. Sarah crossed to her; the diaphanous gown moved like water around her. Natalie heard the small sigh of appreciation.

"Oh, Beth, it's beautiful. I love how you painted the full moon. Do I really look like that?"

"Better." Beth put her arm around Sarah. "Do you truly like it?"

"I love it." Sarah cupped Beth's face in her hands. "I love you."

Natalie saw the sweet expression on Beth's face and it tugged at her heart. When Sarah tipped her head to kiss her, she nearly sighed out loud. They were so obviously in love.

Sarah continued to kiss Beth while she steered her to the maroon chaise against the wall. The back of Beth's knees hit the edge and she sat. Sarah knelt on the floor in front of her and unbuttoned the painter's smock. Beth held still until she was finished then slipped it off her shoulders, revealing the lack of undergarments.

Sarah chuckled. "You're naked, love."

Beth's cheeks flushed. "You told me to be."

"So I did," Sarah answered. She kissed a freckled shoulder before lowering her head to draw a pink nipple into her mouth.

Natalie's sharp intake of breath matched Beth's. She had a perfect view of the pair now. She could feel her own nipples harden in response to the scene in front of her and a wave of desire swept over her. She closed her eyes and felt a small twinge of voyeuristic guilt for witnessing what was a very private moment.

Beth's soft sigh from across the room had Natalie looking back again. Sarah trailed tiny kisses along Beth's stomach before spreading her thighs. Sarah's nightgown pooled on the floor beneath her.

Natalie didn't think she'd ever seen anything so erotic in her life. It was like watching a beautifully choreographed dance. Sarah kissed the softness in front of her and Natalie sighed in tandem with Beth again. She put a hand to her mouth to hush herself. When Sarah's tongue slid along Beth's swollen flesh, she raised her own hips.

Natalie slipped her hand under the waistband of her shorts, surprised to find herself soaking wet. She heard unmistakable sucking sounds and Beth's little whimpers. She found her own clit swollen and engorged, and when she ran her fingers over it, her stomach clenched.

Beth's hips rocked against Sarah's face, her hands twined her long hair. She threw her head back and exposed her long neck before her body stiffened and she fell backward, still panting. Sarah laid her head on her quivering stomach. Her nightgown was pulled up and her hands cupped her sex.

Natalie watched two of her fingers disappear into the wet folds and mirrored her movements.

Beth wrapped Sarah's hair into a tail to pull her face up then sucked her tongue in the rhythm Sarah was dancing between her thighs.

The sight was so unbelievably sensual; Natalie increased her own pressure and tempo until she was gasping for breath. She cried out loud when the orgasm overtook her. Her eyes closed for a moment.

Natalie woke to the sound of heavy footsteps in the hall. *Damn it.* She could also still hear the echo of Sarah and Beth making love. The dream was so real. The noise in the hall stopped and Natalie held her breath, waiting for the door to open. She let it out slowly when nothing happened. She wondered briefly if she should ask her mother if she heard the footsteps and run to her bedroom as she did when she was a child. The silence was almost as unnerving as the footsteps.

A voice in the room whispered. “I will love you forever.”

Chapter Ten

Natalie smelled bacon frying. She found her mother in the kitchen making breakfast and her laptop open on the table. "You've been busy this morning."

Her mother looked up from the stove. "Good morning, sleepyhead. I've been up for hours. Sit. I'll bring you some coffee."

"You don't have to wait on me, Mom." Natalie sat anyway, knowing it was useless to argue with her. "How did you sleep?"

"Oh," her mother said nonchalantly, "I slept fine."

Natalie had a moment of trepidation and hoped like hell her mother didn't have any sex dreams. Oh. God. Now the image was stuck in her head. "Please tell me you didn't have any dreams."

Her mother patted her hand. "No, no funny dreams. Honestly? I felt the dark energy pacing the halls most of the night. How about you?"

Natalie hesitated. "I had dreams that were very vivid. I felt as if I were in the same room with them."

"Who?"

"Sarah and Beth."

Her mother's eyes widened. "Who's Beth?"

"Apparently, she's my doppelganger. The first dreams I had, I was looking out of her eyes with my thoughts." She shivered. "It's more than a little creepy."

Natalie told her mother about witnessing Beth paint the portrait of Sarah, currently hanging above the fireplace. She left out a great deal of the details, but told enough to convey the depth of love they held for each other. She finished her story with how she woke up to the footsteps in the hallway.

"Well, that almost validates my theory that I had about them being trapped." Her mother looked thoughtful and tapped her chin.

"Right before I went back to sleep, I heard one of them say, '*I'll love you forever.*' Mom, it was so real and Beth looked so much like me, it was uncanny." Natalie felt hopeful. "It can't be that simple, right? The connection, I mean."

"One thing I know about spirits, honey, is that it is almost never simple. We can go to the courthouse and library today to search the old-fashioned way for past owners of record."

"I think I know an easier way." Natalie pulled the laptop closer to bring up the online listings for Bayside. She found the number she was looking for and dialed.

"Stan?"

"Yes, this is him."

"Hello. This is Natalie, the one who bought the Seeley place?"

There was a pause on the line. "Yes, Natalie. What can I help you with?"

"Stan, I was hoping you could tell me the names of the previous owners."

"I'm sure that Karen—"

Natalie cut him off. "Please, Stan. You told me yourself how the gossip mill grinds." At this point she was thinking that if Karen hadn't been forthcoming before she bought the house, Natalie didn't trust her to be now. "I just need a name. They did such a tremendous amount of renovation here; they must have come into your store a thousand times."

Another long pause had Natalie wondering if he hung up on her. Then she heard the rustle of papers.

"Okay," he said. "Beecher, Brad and Tina. That's Beecher with two e's."

"Thank you, Stan. I appreciate it."

"Yeah, well. Just don't tell 'em where you got it." His voice was gruff. "Later, Miss Natalie."

"Good-bye," she said to the click.

Her mother checked the listings and found a Beecher, B & T, in a town only thirty miles away. "It's not a common name," she said.

Natalie agreed and keyed the address into the GPS on her phone. "Well, it's a beautiful day for a drive up the coast."

Her mother smiled. "Isn't it just?"

❖

Natalie turned in her seat to look at her mother. "Should we have called?" It seemed like a good idea at the time to surprise the Beechers, but now that they were sitting in the driveway, she was having second thoughts. "Maybe they both work." Natalie was always forgetting that not everyone worked from home.

"Brand new subdivision," her mother said. "Nice house. Not quite as big as the one they left behind, though."

Natalie was too nervous to look at the details. She wanted to get this over with. "Ready?"

The front door opened before they reached it and a woman in her mid-fifties was looking out of the small gap.

"Can I help you?"

"Mrs. Beecher?"

"Yes."

"My name is Natalie and this is my mother, Colleen."

The woman's eyes narrowed. "Are you trying to sell me something or make me come to Jesus?"

There was no easy way to do this, so Natalie jumped right in. "I bought your house." She watched a flicker of fear pass over Mrs. Beecher's face. "We just want to ask you a few questions."

"I've been almost expecting this." She looked resigned as she opened the door wider. "The house was on the market for almost three years, so we were surprised when it sold. Come in then. Can I get you anything?"

"No, thank you, Mrs. Beecher."

"Tina, please. I'm going to need something to drink. Sit down; I'll be right back." She led them to a formal living room.

"She's pale and scared," Natalie's mother said in a low voice. "But she seems very pleasant."

"At least she didn't shut the door in our face or pretend she didn't know why we were here." Natalie was relieved.

Tina returned with three glasses of ice water on a small tray. "You might need it," she said.

Natalie's mother took one. "Thank you, dear. Can you tell us about the house?"

"How did you come to buy it?" Tina asked.

Natalie smiled at the memory. "It was the easiest thing I've ever done in my life. I had been visiting my friend Mary in Bayside. I was driving back up the coast when I saw the sign. I don't know why exactly, but I turned and went straight up to the house. The realtor listed sent Karen up to let me in. I fell in love with the charming old house." She sat back. "And you?"

Tina smiled almost wistfully. "Oh, I did too. Fell in love with it at first sight. My husband was dead set against it. He said it was too much work. But I badgered him until he gave in. I wanted a project, you see. I had empty nest syndrome something awful and thought I needed a project."

"I can understand that," Natalie's mother said.

"The house had been empty for years when we bought it, but the owners before us had replaced all the old plumbing and wiring. Some of the rooms were down to the studs. The kitchen was horrid." Tina shuddered.

"Did you ever talk with them?" Natalie asked.

"No. It was all done through the agency. It was months later after living with the strange events for a while when we thought about asking them. We never did find them." Tina sipped her water and continued.

"It was just awful living in a construction zone." She lowered her voice. "My husband isn't very handy."

Natalie's mother laughed. "I understand that as well."

"We hired a contractor for the big jobs. I had seriously underestimated the size of my little project. They make it look so easy on those decorating shows, don't they? I had visions of painting and decorating to create a showpiece."

"The house is gorgeous. You did an amazing job with it."

Tina's eyes filled. "It is, isn't it?"

She looked so sad, Natalie regretted to ask the next question. She cleared her throat. "You said that strange things happened?"

Tina looked down at her hands. "It all sounds so crazy."

"It's all right. We're not here to judge you."

Tina studied their faces. "Okay. At first, there were strange noises. I could swear I heard someone walking in the hallway. My husband told me it was merely the sounds that old houses make. I didn't make a great deal about it. He was quick to remind me that it was my choice to live there." Tina paused. "I hated the basement, just hated it. Every time I went into it I felt I was being watched. It was a dreadful feeling."

Natalie thought she might not want to hear anymore. She really didn't want to be scared in what was *her* house now.

"Then the knocking in the walls started. Doors would open and shut at odd times. Brad never experienced any of it. He didn't believe me." Her eyes pleaded with them.

"We believe you." Natalie's mother reached over and patted Tina's arm.

"The renovation took almost a year. While it was going on, Brad had explanations for everything. The workman must have done whatever it was that happened to frighten me at the time." Tina waved her hand. "I would show him the articles I found online about hauntings and how renovations stirred up spirits and such."

"It pisses them off."

Tina looked at Natalie's mother. "Thank you. He refused to believe anything that I showed him."

Natalie was beginning to develop a strong dislike for Brad. "That must have been frustrating for you."

"Oh, he's not a bad man, my husband, just very practical. He sees everything in black and white. There are no gray areas for him."

Natalie couldn't imagine what Tina must have felt. She grew up with a mystical mother and grandmother. No one had ever laughed at her, told her that her imagination was stupid or the boogeyman didn't live under her bed. Her mother simply came in and kicked spirit ass with her prayers and crystals. She felt a surge of appreciation for her.

"I thought I was losing my mind. I was the only one who heard things. I lived in terror in my own home and no one believed me."

"Did you have any dreams?" Natalie was curious to how Beth and Sarah fit into this story.

Tina shivered slightly. "Yes. They started at the beginning of the second year we were there. I was always being chased by a large man wearing black. He was horrible. I was convinced he was the one haunting the house. He had this really evil laugh." Tina mimicked the sound.

Natalie's hair rose on the back of her neck and she looked over at her mother. The dark man.

"He would describe the evil things he would do to me if he ever caught me." Tina's face paled.

Natalie sat forward. "Then what happened?"

"My new psychiatrist put me on medication. That stopped the nightmares at least. I walked around doped up for the next several months."

"Oh, you poor thing," Natalie's mother said. "When did you decide to leave?"

"Brad started to have dreams. He didn't want to tell me at first, they were so bad. He started asking me questions about my experiences for the first time. He read the research I had done on the paranormal. Things started to escalate after that, but I was so grateful to know I wasn't the only one experiencing it anymore. My husband had such a hard time accepting all of it. It shook the very foundations of everything he had been taught to believe.

"On the last night we were there, he woke up from a nightmare." Tina choked up a little but continued in a hoarse voice. "And he tried to strangle me."

"Omigod." Natalie was shocked. She hadn't expected to hear that.

"He said he snapped out of it when my eyes turned glassy." She held a hand to her throat. "My husband is a gentle man. In thirty years he never even raised a hand in anger. Anyway, he apologized and cried then told me to pack a bag. He didn't have to tell me twice. At that point, we'd been there for about eighteen months. It was the worst experience of my life. I didn't care that we were leaving, I was so relieved.

"We threw a couple of suitcases together and I was waiting for Brad on the landing when I was pushed from behind. He said he saw the force of it as I was standing a good three feet from the stairs at the time. He raced to me at the bottom, picked me up in one swoop, and rushed me to the hospital.

"We were scared to death. The emergency room doctor said I was lucky I didn't break my neck. I came out of that hospital with two cracked ribs and a broken ankle and I considered myself lucky."

That did it. Natalie was scared now. "It sounds terrifying. I'm so sorry for dredging up such horrible memories."

"But you've had experiences yourself or you wouldn't have found me, right?"

"Your husband's dreams?" Natalie's mother reminded her gently.

"He finally told me months later. He said he had very vivid dreams of beating me, punishing me. He couldn't say for what, but that he knew he began to enjoy it. The sight of my blood turned him on. After the night he tried to kill me, he'd had enough. It was all real then. We only went back to pack, in broad daylight, and with a group of people.

"We bought this brand new house and Brad never said a word to me about paying two mortgages for the last three years. We pretend it never happened on the surface. I'm sorry to tell you how ecstatic we were when it sold." Tina looked down.

Natalie tried to take it all in. The Beechers had a horrifying experience, but it didn't resemble her own. "What about the women?"

Tina looked genuinely puzzled. "What women? There's only one. The dark man."

"You never smelled lavender or dreamt of Beth and Sarah?"

"No." Tina shook her head.

Natalie didn't want to go into the details. Tina had been through enough sharing her experience. Instead, she steered the conversation in another direction. "Did you do research on the Seeleys? Maybe to find out who the dark man was?"

"I always meant to. You have to remember that I thought I was going crazy. I wasn't looking for any specific information. After we left, I didn't care. I wanted to erase that part of my life." She looked contrite. "I never even thought about how I was passing the nightmare to someone else. I am so sorry."

Natalie thought that Tina looked a bit frail. She didn't have it in her to say anything that would make her feel guilty. It wasn't in her nature. Her heart only wanted to reassure Tina it was fine. She would let the Beechers close this chapter of their lives. "Well," she said finally. "The good news is that I appear to have different ghosts."

"Good girl," Natalie's mother murmured.

Natalie didn't mention the dark man. She told her instead about the feminine energy in the house. The look of relief on Tina's face told Natalie she'd done the right thing.

Her mother, bless her heart, helped to put Tina at ease then they thanked her for her time.

It wasn't until they were nearly home that Natalie realized she hadn't remembered to ask about the painting. She doubted Tina would have known about it. After all, Natalie watched it being created in her dream. She was curious as to where it was hiding all these years. It seemed she had more questions than answers than ever before.

"Mom?"

"I don't know yet, sweetheart."

"I didn't ask you anything yet."

Her mother smiled. "Yes, you did."

"Not out loud, I didn't."

"I know." Natalie's mother looked out the window. "We have more research to do."

"To find Sarah and Beth?"

"Yes and the dark man who controls the house. Let's put it away for now, okay? Besides, don't you have a date to get ready for?"

Natalie immediately felt butterflies in her stomach. She was excited to see Van. Yes, she could put this on the back burner for tonight.

Tonight, she was going to explore new possibilities.

❖

Get a grip! You're thirty-two, not fourteen! Natalie heard the front door slam and the sound of feet running up the stairs and down the hall. Mary burst in her room without bothering to knock.

"Am I too late? Do you have any idea what it's like to take thirty-five teenagers to the museum? Fricking teenagers can drive a sane woman to drink. What are you going to wear? Are you going to kiss her?"

Natalie grabbed Mary by the arms. "It's all about me right this second, Mare. Help me. What *does* one wear on a first date? It's hardly fair. I haven't been on a date in thirteen years, and even back then I never cared what I *wore.* What if I commit some horrible lesbian faux pas on my first date with a woman?"

Mary started to laugh, but cut it off abruptly when Natalie glared at her. "What do you have?"

Natalie flung her arm toward the bed. It was covered in a pile nearly two feet deep. "Every piece of clothing that I own is on that bed. I've tried it all on. None of my clothes look right."

"Nat? You better think of something, because she's here and you're in your underwear." Mary looked over to her. "Nice fancy underwear, I might add, yet nonetheless, not appropriate for dinner wear."

"I think I'm going to throw up." Natalie bent over and put a hand over her stomach. "I'm so nervous. What's she wearing?"

Mary gave a little wave out the window. "Black 501s, with a black short sleeved shirt tucked in. Oh, and she's wearing shit kickers. Damn, girl, if I weren't straight, I'd want her. She's hot!"

Natalie groaned and dove back into the mess on the bed. Mary hurried over to help and finally held up a green Gypsy-style summer dress that laced up the front.

"Matches your eyes, easy on hers, it's perfect." She left the room to answer the front door.

Twenty minutes later, Natalie headed for the voices in the kitchen. She took a deep breath, smoothed her hair, and breezed in the door. "Sorry I kept you waiting." She was so nervous, her heart thumped almost painfully.

Van was sitting in one of the kitchen chairs with her long legs straight out in front of her. "You look great."

Two hours straightening my hair and doing my makeup. But wasn't that look just worth it. "Thank you, Van. So do you."

Van smiled. "Thanks. I was just getting ready to tell your mother and Mary that one of my ancestors worked here when the house was originally built."

Natalie saw her mother's eyebrows rise and jumped in. "Wow. In all the excitement around here, did I forget to mention that?"

"What excitement?" Van asked.

"The house is haunted," Mary blurted.

Natalie winced inwardly. Great, now Van would think she was nuts. She looked anxiously over to see her reaction.

"Really?" Van looked around the kitchen. "I've heard the rumors. What's going on?"

"You're not surprised?" asked Natalie.

Van laughed. "Hey, I watch *Ghost Adventures.*"

Natalie was grateful for the humor. She didn't want to talk about it anymore today. She was nervous enough as it was. "Shall we?" she asked Van then caught herself from sighing when she stood up next to her. She felt her nerve endings fire up and a skip in her pulse. She could only hope she didn't make an ass of herself tonight.

Van led Natalie to the truck and admired how amazing she looked in that dress. She no longer questioned her motive for asking her out. She looked delicious.

"There's no graceful way to do this in a dress. Is there?" Natalie asked when she stood in front of the high cab.

"Nope." Van chuckled. "Pretty much, none." She helped Natalie up and then went around and jumped in the driver's side. "I hope you like seafood. My uncle's family owns a restaurant on the boardwalk. Are you okay with that?"

"I love seafood. I'm sure it will be wonderful."

During the short ride down the coast, Van was quiet but kept darting glances over at Natalie. She looked adorable sitting there with her hands folded primly in her lap. When she realized that Natalie seemed to be waiting for her to talk, Van searched for her long-dormant flirting skills. She hadn't needed them for a long time. "I love your work," she said finally.

Natalie smiled. "Thank you. Did you visit the Web page?"

Van nodded. "Here we are." She pulled smoothly into the crowded parking lot of the restaurant.

"Which-fish?" asked Natalie.

Van chuckled. "Uncle John couldn't decide on a name for the first year. He would just shout out, 'Which fish do you want?' So my aunt had a sign made. Over the years, the place became so popular that they expanded and dispensed with the counter. The name stuck, though."

Van helped Natalie step down and felt her slight tremble. It touched her. Then it dawned on her that this was a real date. She'd grown so used to casual pick-ups and booty calls that only required small talk that she didn't know quite what to think at the moment. And when Natalie smiled at her, she lost the ability to think much at all.

"Vanessa!" her uncle's voice boomed from right next to her. "It's so good to see you." Van turned to warn Natalie, but she was too slow. Her uncle was already pumping her arm in his naturally exuberant way.

"And who is this?"

"Natalie, this is my uncle, John." The words were hardly out of her mouth before Van was engulfed in a bear hug before he stood back and beamed at her.

"It's been a long time since you've brought a friend. Go and sit at the family table." He pointed outside to the large deck behind the wall of windows in the back. "Your aunt will be so happy to see you."

Van led Natalie to a table overlooking the water. In the center of the weathered wood was a large engraved plaque bearing the name Easton.

"Oh, cute," Natalie said. "Family table as in literally."

"My aunt said if they were going to work so hard during meal times, there had to be a permanent table for us. She also said it had to be the best in the house."

"It's certainly beautiful here. The sky looks like it's on fire and getting ready to fall into the ocean."

Aunt Becky put a basket of French bread in front of them and kissed Van's cheek before chuckling.

"Don't tell me," Van said. "I've grown another inch."

Her aunt laughed and winked at Natalie. "We thought she would never stop growing. She's taller than both my sons."

"Meaner too," said Van.

"Oh, you are not." Natalie's eyes widened slightly. "Are you?"

"My cousin Rory certainly thinks so. I broke his nose in the seventh grade."

"Ryan still insists it was your idea to steal your uncle's car to go joyriding in." Her aunt's tone was teasing.

"Geez," Van said. "That was more than twenty years ago. Isn't there some statute of limitations for that?"

Her aunt patted her shoulder. "Absolutely not. I'll go get your wine."

"It must have been wonderful to grow up in a large family. Do you have any brothers or sisters?"

"No. My dad has four brothers and three of them have ten kids between them. They all stayed in this area, and me and the cousins grew up together." Van buttered a piece of the bread and handed it to Natalie. "You?"

"Only child." Natalie sighed. "I always wanted a sibling."

"Well, Natalie. The Eastons are legion. If you ever need something built, need a cop, a priest, or if you're hungry, we are your go-tos."

"What about a landscaper?" Natalie teased. "Who do I call?"

Van winked at her. "That, you already have." She realized how much she was enjoying the flirtation and she felt a small twinge of guilt. The whole purpose of bringing Natalie to the family restaurant was for the buffer she thought it would create. She anticipated the interruptions, thinking that they would keep things from getting too intimate. Natalie laughed at something Uncle John said. Van hadn't considered beforehand how easily Natalie would fit in.

"They like you," she said when her aunt left for the third time. Van felt a knock in her chest when Natalie locked eyes with her. The red sunset behind her had faded into an indigo dusk and the candles flickered soft light on her face.

"I'm having a wonderful time, Van." Natalie looked down and Van could see the blush stain her cheeks.

She reached out and took her hand. "What are we doing here, Natalie?" Van was insanely attracted to her, but feeling what she considered to be very dangerous emotions. Ones that she'd buried a long time ago. Van had always been very honest with the women she took home with her: her heart was off-limits.

Natalie sat back and neatly put the napkin on her plate. "That was amazing. I'm so full. Can we go for a walk on the beach?"

Van smiled. "Of course. Let's go say good-bye first, or I'll never hear the end of it."

They used the steps from the rear deck to access the sandy beach. Natalie admired the flowers spilling out of cobalt blue planters. The rhythm of the waves and the lights of the boardwalk gave the beach a magical feeling to her. She knew she would remember this night forever.

She took off her heels and stood on the bottom step, which put her at Van's eye level. She stared at her lips. Were they as soft as they looked? Natalie held very still and the desire she saw mirrored in Van's eyes quickened her pulse. She was finding it difficult to breathe normally. Anticipation seemed to close her throat and she couldn't find any words. The emotion was so intense; she closed her eyes for a second.

Van gently pressed her lips against hers and Natalie's immediate reaction was, yes, they were as soft as they looked. Then Van wrapped her arms around her and Natalie felt the heat of the full body contact. She heard herself whimper, and her knees went weak. She tightened her grip on Van's shoulders.

It was Van who broke the kiss first and she laid her forehead against Natalie's, her breath a hot caress on Natalie's cheek. It was the most spectacular kiss she'd ever had. She could feel her heart knock against Van's breasts which were pressed into her own.

Natalie felt shy but not awkward. Kissing Van felt like the most natural thing in the world.

Van lifted Natalie off the step, into the soft sand, and took her hand. Van hadn't expected that kiss would shake her up the way it did. The emotion that welled up in her chest surprised her. She'd felt her heart rattle the cage she'd carefully built around it. Instinct had her stepping back a little. She needed some space, and hearing Natalie's story could provide that.

Natalie hadn't spoken yet. It wasn't until they reached the water's edge that Van asked her. "Why are you here?"

"Here with you, or here in Bayside?"

Van shrugged. "Both."

"Do you want the whole story or the abridged version?"

"Whichever you want to tell me."

Natalie sighed. "I'm not going to go into great detail about my divorce just yet. Suffice it to say that it was the reason I moved here. This evening has been perfect and we'll leave details for another time."

Van nodded.

"I'm here with you because I want to be."

The answer was so matter-of-fact and honest that Van decided to be direct. "Are you a lesbian, Natalie?"

"I'm pretty certain I am."

Natalie looked so shy Van softened her approach and whispered in her ear. "Have you ever made love with another woman?"

"Well, not technically."

Van chuckled. "What exactly does that mean?"

This time it was Natalie who stepped back. "Okay. I'll tell you the whole story. It only makes sense when it's all put together in context."

They walked along the water and Van listened as Natalie talked. She didn't interrupt her while she told her about her life with Jason. Van's mind raced with the implications of a rebound relationship. Then she caught herself. When did *that* start to matter? When had her mind gone to relationship status? Somewhere over the shrimp cocktail?

When Natalie was done, Van tilted her chin up. "Let me get this straight. You were married to an asshole who called you frigid for twelve years. Then you move here where you started to have sexy dreams about making love with women and decided you're a lesbian."

Natalie blushed. "Well, yes."

"And you want me to be your first lover?" Van hesitated when she felt a tug over her heart. Natalie was sweet and looked gorgeous in the moonlight. She didn't know if she would be able to walk away from her after she made love to her. Being someone's first was a huge responsibility, and she already cared enough about Natalie to not want to hurt her. Van needed to walk away now. She wanted to tell her that they could be friends, she really did. But what came out of her mouth was completely different. "So, Natalie, do you want to come home with me?"

❖

Natalie leaned against the closed door and tried not to feel stupid. She just had the best date in her life with the gorgeous Van, whom she was fiercely attracted to. Oh, and a kiss that rocked her world, let's not forget that.

"So, Natalie, do you want to come home with me?"

She wanted to do just that. But what did she do instead? She looked straight into Van's eyes and froze. Jason's ugly words came out of nowhere to slap her. *Frigid.*

Natalie knew her body was telling her the complete opposite, but to erase something that had been a huge part of her identity for her entire adult life was at the very least, difficult. She felt a piece of her would die if she went home with Van and saw disappointment, or worse, regret, in her face the next morning.

Van took her refusal seemingly in stride and was pleasant to her on the way home. The kiss she gave Natalie on the cheek was a friendly one, giving no hint of the passion they had felt earlier.

Natalie went to her room, stepping quietly through the hall so as not to wake her sleeping mother and got ready for bed.

She lay still but her emotions wouldn't settle and her mind raced with alternate scenarios that could have played out, but didn't. She felt the threat of tears burning behind her eyes.

What if Van didn't want to go out with her again? Natalie didn't know if her heart could take another rejection.

As she slipped into a dream state, Natalie became conscious she was running. While she sped down the hallway, it seemed to extend itself, the stairway slipping farther and farther away. The only sound she could hear was the echo of solid footsteps behind her. Even those sounded far away as her heavy breathing and heartbeat pounded in her eardrums. She could see Beth running beside her in slow motion, terror etched in her face as she looked back.

"Go ahead and run, you stupid little bitch. I'll catch you. You're going to wish you hadn't."

Chapter Eleven

Van felt completely useless this morning. She couldn't concentrate. Maybe she should go out with a work crew to get her mind on the job and off of Natalie and the abrupt ending of their date last night. She headed outside intending to do just that, but jumped into her truck instead. Van turned into the now familiar driveway then dialed her phone.

"Hello?"

"Natalie?"

"Yes. Who's calling please?"

God, she had a sexy voice. "It's Van. Did I wake you?"

"No."

"I called to see if you would have coffee with me this morning."

"I would love to. What time?"

"Great. Open your front door." She snapped her phone closed.

"You have me at a slight disadvantage here." Natalie gestured to her rumpled nightshirt and messy hair.

Van thought she looked adorable. She wanted to pick her up and crawl back in bed with her. "You look beautiful in the morning." She stopped and sniffed the air. "Is that *pot* I smell?"

"What?" Natalie shook her head and laughed. "No, it's sage. We were doing a house cleansing."

Van saw Natalie's mother in the hallway holding an abalone shell and large feather. She smiled at her before disappearing into the hall. She pulled Natalie into a hug and kissed her. "Good morning."

"Mmm. Good morning. Are you hungry? My mother made muffins."

"Muffins and ghost chasing? You've been busy. I've already eaten." She sat at the table, accepted the coffee cup and stared at her over the rim. The air sizzled and her stomach muscles tightened when Natalie nervously licked her lips. "I'm sorry that I came on so strong last night."

"God. It wasn't you. Please don't think it was you." Natalie stood next to her and Van pulled her into her lap. She fit perfectly and Van couldn't resist nuzzling her neck.

"I thought you wouldn't want to see me again," Natalie said.

"Oh, I want to see you, little one." *I want to see every inch of you.*

Natalie smiled. "I'm so glad that you do." Her mother came into the kitchen and turned back around. "Come back here, Mom."

Van was sorry when Natalie stood. Her legs burned from the contact and her jeans felt too tight.

"I don't want to interrupt anything." Natalie's mother put the shell and feather on the table. "But I'm all done."

Van was going to ask about the cleansing but a voice erupted from her hip.

"That sounds familiar, what's the title of that tune?"

"Take this job and shove it."

Natalie laughed. "You did not."

"It's the foreman on my crew, Rick. I have to take this. Excuse me."

Natalie watched her leave the room.

"You're staring at her ass."

"Mother!"

"Well, you are. Just saying." Her mother laughed.

The moment felt almost surreal. Never in a million years did Natalie think she would be discussing the finer aspects of such a lovely *female* ass with her mother. "Okay, I was."

The phone on the wall rang. "It's your father." Her mother got up to answer it.

How does she do that? She knew it would be her father. Her mother was never wrong. Natalie took the opportunity at having them both on the phone to run upstairs and at least brush her hair. Maybe she could touch up her face and put some clothes on. Natalie looked at the unmade bed. Or, she thought, get Van naked. She shook her head. Not with her mother in the house.

The smell of burning sage was stronger in her room. Natalie truly hoped it would work and chase the dark man away. She didn't want another nightmare like she had last night. At the same time, she hoped the cleansing didn't chase Beth and Sarah away. She felt attached to them.

When she came back down, Van was standing by the front door. "I'm sorry, I have to go."

Natalie was disappointed. "Something for work?"

Van nodded. "Irate client that wants to talk to the boss. For once, I'm sorry to say that would be me."

Natalie slipped her arms around Van's waist then tilted her head back to see her face. "Well, a girl's gotta do what a girl's gotta do. And I have to do this." Natalie drew her arms around Van's neck and pulled her down to kiss her softly. Once, twice, three times until Van wrapped her hands in Natalie's hair to pull her closer.

Natalie sighed. "Oh, yes. More please." Van's tongue flicked across her lips and Natalie felt the heat race straight to her core. She wanted to climb up Van's body to wrap her legs around her waist then fall to the floor. She wanted to lick, taste, and bite her neck. Every nerve ending in her body snapped to attention and her pulse raced. Natalie felt gloriously alive.

The fiery kiss had taken on a life of its own, becoming a vortex—spinning with passion and desire. Van staggered and let go of Natalie's hair so she could brace herself from falling.

"Fuck it," Van said when her phone rang again.

The remark surprised a weak laugh from Natalie. She panted in an effort to breathe. She felt drunk and her heart was racing faster than she could ever remember. Was this normal? She realized she didn't care; she only wanted to do it again. A lot. "You need to go," she said. "Boss."

"You can be the boss of me later."

Natalie almost purred. "'Kay."

Van brushed a hand down Natalie's cheek. "I'm not going to kiss you again because then I'll never leave. Dinner tonight?"

"What time?"

"Around six thirty? Oh, and I almost forgot. Your mother and I were talking about the house when you were upstairs and she mentioned that you were going to the library today?"

Natalie nodded.

"Hold off on that. I called my dad and he said he knows some of the history. He invited you both to dinner tomorrow night."

"We'd love to come."

Van smiled at her. "Bye, Natalie. I'll see you later."

Van called her father to let him know that Natalie and her mother accepted his invitation for dinner. She could still smell Natalie's perfume. It was as heady and intoxicating as Natalie was herself.

When she arrived at the job site, she saw the crew loading equipment and her foreman standing by his truck. He was yelling into his phone then closed it when he saw Van.

"Great," Van said under her breath when she recognized the anger on Rick's face. He was pissed.

"That woman." He hissed then pointed to the house.

Van searched her mental file. "Miss Alora," she corrected him.

"Whatever. She was a sweetheart when we arrived. We started work and the woman came out screaming like she was demon-possessed."

Van got out of her truck and sighed. "What happened?"

"Every plant, every tree, every single goddamn flower was *not* what she ordered."

Van interrupted. "You have a signed estimate and contract."

"And I tried to show it to her. She insisted on seeing you."

"Okay. Where's the paperwork?"

"Not necessary. She fired us '*cheatin' sumbitches*' and ordered us off her property. Then she called—"

"The cops." Van finished for him when she saw her cousin Rory pull up in his Bayside City Police Department cruiser.

"Are you ripping off little old ladies again, Vanessa?"

"Bite me, Rory."

"Look," he said. "I'm going to get out of my car and look like I'm reading you the riot act. Then you can look properly chastised and leave, okay?"

Van turned to Rick. "Did you dig anything up yet?"

"No, we were done marking out boundaries and loaded in all the stock. It's all back in the trucks now."

Van checked her watch. "Okay, tell the crew to go back to the nursery. I have another job you can go to after lunch." She wrote down Natalie's address. "You can start in on the brush clean up. I'll be up later with the plans and we can go over them then." Rick nodded at her and left.

She turned back to her cousin. "Give it to me, officer."

Rory made a big show of his lecture, gesturing and pointing toward Miss Alora who was looking out her window. "Miss Alora is a paranoid schizophrenic and must be off her meds again." Rory paced in front of Van. "She calls us at least three times a week to report her neighbors and the government spies in her bushes."

Van hung her head and got back in her truck, biting her lip to keep from laughing.

"One more thing," Rory yelled at her.

"Yes?"

He winked at her. "I heard about the girl." Rory slapped the side of her truck. "Now, you can leave."

"Yes, sir!" Van said.

❖

Natalie sat across from her mother at the table.

"I'm going to love Van simply because she put that look on my baby's face."

"I can't seem to stop smiling."

"When are you going to see her again?"

"Tonight," Natalie said. "What do you want to do now that we're not going to the library?"

"You could rest, Nat. You had a rough night."

Natalie had forgotten the nightmare until her mother brought it up. Of course, she thought, Van was an awesome distraction. She shook her head. "We did the house cleansing. That should work, right?"

"The energy seems lighter in here. I don't feel any negativity around. Do you want to unpack some boxes?"

"No, I really don't. Let's go shopping instead."

Natalie's mother grabbed her purse and beat her to the front door. Her mother loved to shop. It was something you never had to ask her twice. Natalie gave her phone to her mother when they were in the car. "Here. Call Mary and have her meet us."

Natalie and her mother browsed a gift shop while they waited. When Mary arrived they walked to her favorite boutique.

"How come you didn't call me this morning to give me deets?"

"I'm sorry, Mary. I had a horrible nightmare last night, and when I got up Mom suggested we do the house cleansing immediately."

"We can get back to that. I want to hear about your date."

Natalie smiled. "It was wonderful. I had an amazing time."

"Yeah, yeah. And?"

"And what?"

Mary looked exasperated. "You're killing me here, Nat. *And* where did she take you? *And* what did you talk about. *And* did you sleep with her?"

"That's a lot of *ands*," Natalie's mother said.

"Please give me some crumbs." Mary ticked a list off on her fingers. "One, I've been married for twenty years. Two, my twin sons are going through puberty. Three, all the men in the house play sports. Do I really need to tell you about laundry day? Because—"

"Okay, okay." Natalie laughed. "We went to that restaurant." She pointed.

"Which-fish?"

"Van's uncle and aunt own it."

"Nice. They have great food." Mary held the door for her. "Now answer the big one."

"No, I did not." Natalie paused. "Yet."

Mary's face fell. "That's just sad. I was hoping to get some vicarious thrills."

"I'm seeing her again tonight."

"There is hope after all," Mary said. "Oooh, shoes!" She beelined for the wall display.

"She's easily distracted, isn't she?" asked Natalie's mother.

"It's part of her charm," Natalie said to the empty space beside her. She turned and saw her mother racing to the purses on the opposite wall. She laughed and shook her head. "As it is yours."

Natalie slipped the soft blue dress over her head and smoothed it down. She turned in the four-way mirror, noticing that the dress hugged every curve. She had never owned one so short in the past, but since this appeared to be a time of trying new things, she figured what the hell. She opened the dressing room door so she could model for her mother and Mary. Two young women squeezing into the room next to her nearly knocked her over.

"Oh, Nat. It's beautiful on you."

"Do you think? Is it too short?" She spun in a slow circle.

Mary shook her head. "No. I'd love to see the look on Van's face when she sees nothing but leg."

The giggling stopped behind them and the door latch clicked. A young blond woman, maybe in her mid-twenties, peeked out. "Did you say Van? Van Easton?"

Natalie turned. "Yes."

The woman snickered. "She won't care about the dress. You'll be lucky if she remembers your name the day after." Her friend poked her head out as well and giggled.

She appraised Natalie. "Besides, aren't you a little old for her?"

Mary shifted so she was closer to the pair. Natalie knew it was because Mary felt she was protecting her, but she was going to fight her own battles now. "What are you, twelve?" she asked. "What business is it of yours?"

The woman's face turned ugly. "Oh, I've been all up in Van's business."

"Have you?" Natalie put ice into her voice. "Perhaps it's just *your* name she's forgotten." She went back into her dressing room to take off the dress. She had no clue how to handle this situation, and at the moment couldn't think of another snappy comeback.

"Here kitty, kitty, kitty." The voices sang next door.

Natalie heard the saleswoman tell them to leave, but she could still hear them laughing on their way to the exit. Then she heard her mother's parting shot. "Those jeans you were trying on didn't do a thing to hide your baby fat."

The door slammed when the women left and Natalie came out. She looked at the clerk. "I'll take it," she said. "Mom, Mary, let's go to lunch."

Her mother waited until they were seated in the little café. "Do you want to talk about it?"

"Yeah, let's trash the bitches," Mary said.

"I know, right?" Natalie thought about it. "As tasteless and rude as they may be, I'm not going to let them ruin my day."

"Good girl," said her mother. "We won't talk about the little bitches."

"Mother!"

"Well?" she said. "They were."

"I hate that they planted a seed like that," said Mary.

"What part of I don't want to…Look, we both have pasts. Van's might be a little more colorful than mine, but nonetheless."

The waitress came by for their order then left. "Now," Natalie said. "Let me see what you bought." She laughed when her mother and Mary squealed in unison and reached for their bags.

❖

Van leaned on her shovel and wiped the sweat from the back of her neck. She turned when she heard the sound of a car. Natalie was home. Her stomach did a funny little flip when she saw genuine delight light her eyes. It made this morning's fiasco totally worth the trouble. Van wondered what else she could do for her to keep that look on her face. The sound of chainsaws and trimmers behind her was too loud for conversation, so she pointed to the house. Van followed Natalie and her mother into the foyer where they set their bags down. Natalie gave her a shy kiss. "I thought my yard wasn't slated for a couple of weeks. I'm so excited." Natalie did a little happy dance.

Van thought it was sweet. "We're going to have to test those dance moves tonight."

The smile left Natalie's face. "I'm sorry. I have to cancel our plans. My father called a few minutes ago. He fractured his ankle and my mother is leaving tomorrow."

Van fought her disappointment. "Is he okay?"

"He will be. It's Mom's last night here." Natalie wrapped her arms around Van's waist.

"It's okay, I understand." Van rested her chin on the top of her head. "I'm all sweaty."

"S'okay." The reply was muffled.

Natalie's mother returned from the kitchen. "Tell your father I'm sorry about the dinner. I was looking forward to meeting him."

"We can reschedule for tonight," said Van.

"We don't want to put anyone out on such short notice," Natalie's mother said.

Van flipped her phone from her belt. "Oh, it's not a problem. He's already gone shopping. He's a bit of a show-off in the kitchen and he loves to cook." Van excused herself to make the call.

"Dad says no biggie," she said when she found them in the kitchen.

"That's wonderful," said Natalie right before her mother nodded her assent.

Van smiled. "Great. You can follow me over when we're done here for the day." She could clean up there because she kept clothes in her old room at her father's house. "Would you like to see where we started out here?"

Natalie took Van's outstretched hand. "I'd love to."

❖

Natalie and her mother waited for Van on the wide, comfortable porch when she got waylaid by a customer. "I love this place," said Natalie. "It's so charming."

"Sorry about that." Van led them through the hall. "We're here," she called up the stairs.

"Come in, come in."

Natalie reached the top first. "Hello, sir. I'm Natalie and this is my mother, Colleen." She was struck by how much Van resembled her father.

"It's so nice to meet you." He shook both their hands. "I'm Victor. Please, sit."

"Your place is wonderful," Natalie's mother said.

"Thank you. Now, what can I get you to drink?"

Van excused herself to shower then Natalie sat next to her mother on the sofa. Victor came back in with stuffed mushrooms on a silver tray.

"I love these." Natalie popped one into her mouth.

Her mother took a dainty little bite. "You didn't have to go to all this trouble." She smiled. "But I'm glad you did."

He blushed. "It's not often I have a house full of beautiful women. I heard your husband had an accident? I hope he's okay."

"I appreciate you asking. He'll be fine. I've been telling him to fix that old step for years."

Natalie felt a little rush when Van appeared in the doorway. Her hair was slicked back; she was wearing tight faded jeans and a plain white shirt. Natalie understood in the moment what the term masculine beauty meant. Van was all hard muscle and soft curves at the same time. It made her mouth water. Natalie barely caught herself from sighing out loud, but still couldn't tear her gaze away from Van's.

"Smells good, Dad."

"It's just about done," he said. "We can go ahead and sit in the dining room."

Natalie and her mother helped bring out the food. When they were all seated, Victor began his story without any preamble.

"This is what I know, or have been told over the years. Our family has lived in this area for oh, about five generations. Bayside was little more than a fishing village a hundred years ago. One of the locals, Robert Seeley, moved to San Francisco where he met and married the rich daughter of a man who made a fortune during the gold rush."

He pointed his fork at Natalie. "It was Robert who built your house for his wife. I tried talking to your grandpa, Vanessa. It was not one of his good days. So you might try him later for more details as it was *his* grandpa who worked on the estate."

"My grandpa has Alzheimer's," Van explained.

"I'm so sorry," said Natalie. "That must be so difficult for you."

"He's turning ninety this year. He told us that he's had a wonderful life and if he gets stuck in the past sometimes, it must be because he felt it was worth reliving."

"That's a wonderfully positive way to look at it," said Natalie's mother.

He smiled. "It is. And he insists on it. Now, where was I? Oh, yes, I have to fast forward here. Sometime in the nineteen twenties or so, Richard Seeley, the only son, brought home his wife, Elizabeth. Some said she was no more than a child, maybe fifteen at the most. There was whispering being done behind hands, rumors of assault and brutal violence happening in the home. These were hard times for women in those days when they were little better than property and had no rights. But the servants had their own gossip network and the story was passed down about the rich people up on the cliff."

Natalie was fascinated with the story. When she felt Van's hand grip her own under the table, she had a moment of completeness. That she was in the right place at the right time doing exactly what she wanted. It was an incredible new feeling. She leaned slightly into Van's shoulder. Van's father poured more wine and passed the bottle.

"Now, Richard had the reputation of being a ruthless man with no morals or feelings. According to the servants, Beth never left the house. She was, for all intents and purposes, a prisoner up there and the story is that he beat her without mercy."

"Asshole," Van hissed.

"I'll second that," said Natalie.

Her mother lifted her glass. "Third."

"Goes without saying," he said. "Seems the only friend that poor young Beth had was Sarah, Richard's sister. As an interesting side note and validation for Richard's cruelty, Sarah herself had fled the house the same day she turned eighteen. But she returned for Richard's wedding and stayed for a time. Then Sarah returned to France, where she'd been living."

Natalie drew back, surprised. "You're saying that Sarah left the house?" She looked over to her mother who also had a questioning look on her face. "Sarah left Beth?" Natalie recalled her dream and the deep love they had for each other. That didn't sound right at all, but she kept quiet while Van's father continued.

"No one ever saw her again. Later, around that time, Richard and Beth had a son, Henry. Yes, I believe that's right. Anyway, when he was just a small child, Beth ran away with another man."

"And who could blame her?" asked Van.

"Not me," answered her father. "The servants never believed it and suspected foul play, but there were no official accusations."

"During the time period they lived in, if enough money crossed greedy palms, evil deeds could be hushed quite effectively." Nat's mother nodded.

"Indeed," he said. "After Beth disappeared, Richard closed up the house and moved to New York. The house was empty for years until Richard came back. Town gossip says he returned and shut himself up in the house, never leaving it. According to the locals, he was flat out crazy. Some believed it was guilt that drove him to insanity. It's said that he would stand in the turret room windows and stare at the sea, laughing for hours.

"They found old Richard Seeley dead by the fountain one day, covered in dirt. Henry, the son, never set foot on the property. He sold it through the agency in town. That must have been sometime in the nineteen forties, shortly before I was born.

"Most of this story is all hearsay. After getting the gist of it from my father, I called my brothers and asked them what they remembered as well.

"Over the years, there have been several owners. But it has stood empty more often than not. No one ever stays for long." He paused and considered for a moment. "Well now, Natalie, I hope I'm not scaring you."

She felt a slight chill but laughed anyway. "Oh, we O'Donnells take these things in stride."

Her mother explained. "When my mother visited, we had séances instead of playing bridge."

Natalie missed her Nana, who died when she was nineteen. She and her mother had always accepted the validity of ghosts. No one ever raised even an eyebrow when there was an empty place setting at the dinner table for dead relatives. Sometimes it was a little spooky, but Natalie didn't ever remember being very scared by spirits. Then again, they hadn't been sadistic wife beaters either.

Natalie was still curious as to why Sarah and Beth chose her to play out their story. At this point, she felt a little helpless for them. It's not as if she could change anything while they were alive and living through Richard's reign of terror. She sincerely hoped that the house cleansing had rid the house of his violent energy and that it gave Beth and Sarah some peace. She ignored the prickly feeling on her neck and tried to convince herself.

Van helped clear the table then sat with her father after Natalie and her mother insisted on doing the dinner dishes. "That was a fascinating story, Dad. I had no idea that you knew so much about the mansion."

"Like I said earlier, I talked with your uncles. It turned out that John had the most information and a family tree to boot. I was surprised myself."

"Odd how history slips away from us in such a relatively short period of time, you know?"

"Your Natalie seems like a very nice woman."

Van smiled. "She is."

"You like her."

"I do."

"Really, Vanessa, you need to quit chattering. I can't get a word in edgewise."

"Ha ha, Dad." Van considered what to say. She heard Natalie laugh in the other room and was struck by how comfortable shc felt hearing it. She did like Natalie, very much, and enjoyed her company. Actually, she felt entranced. Van felt a little anxious about the revelation. She hadn't bothered to look beneath the surface of any woman she'd been with in the last six years, and her heart seized a little. She was attracted to Natalie, almost painfully so. But underneath that, Van realized she wanted to know much more about her. That scared her to death.

Natalie came out of the kitchen. "Where's the little girls' room?"

"I'll show you. It's this way." She took Natalie's hand and pulled her into the hallway. Van waited outside the door and when she came out, tugged her into the bedroom across the hall. "Finally," Van said and wrapped her up. "A minute alone with you."

Natalie smiled. "Hmm. Let's not waste it."

Van kissed her, softly at first because she meant to keep it gentle, but desire overtook her intention when Natalie's tongue flicked across her lips. Van caught it and sucked and felt Natalie's knees dip. "You like that?"

She heard a soft little sigh in response. "Yes."

Van held on to Natalie and started to move backward toward the bed, then through her sexual haze realized their parents were in the living room. But it wasn't as if Natalie was fighting it. It took a huge effort on her part, but Van let her go.

"I want you so much, Natalie," Van leaned and whispered in her ear. "But when I take you?"

Natalie's eyes were wide. "When you take me?"

"I want you to be able to scream."

"Oh. My. God," Natalie said. "I repeat, omigod."

Natalie's mother knocked on the door. "Honey? I'm sorry, but we have to go now. My flight is early."

"Okay, Mom. I'll be right there." Natalie kissed Van. "Play date is over."

Van laughed. "I'll walk you out. We're still on for tomorrow, right?"

"Absolutely." Natalie stopped in front of the dresser. Van's high school sports trophies and pictures still littered every available surface. She turned and smiled. "The jock?"

Van laughed. "Yes. Letterman."

Natalie looked sad for a moment. "You wouldn't have looked at me twice. I was the geek."

"You underestimate yourself and me."

Natalie continued to look at the pictures. "And this one?" She pointed to a photo of Cara that was stuck in the mirror frame.

Van paused. "We'll talk more at dinner." She opened the door, steering her away from the picture and into the living room where her mother was waiting and thanking Van's father for the amazing dinner and story.

Van kissed her father's cheek before seeing Natalie and her mother to their car. She wanted to go home and think by herself. Her father would only pepper her with questions if she stayed, and she didn't know if, or how, she was going to answer them yet.

❖

Natalie and her mother talked about what they'd learned when they got home. "I just don't buy that Sarah left."

"Or," her mother said, "that Beth ran off."

"And still, nobody has mentioned being haunted by them." Natalie curled her legs underneath her and sipped her tea. "I mean, why me? Why now? It can't just be that I look like her."

"Beth was a child bride terrorized by a sadistic husband who apparently abused his sister, Sarah, as well. It doesn't seem farfetched that they would find love for each other."

Natalie recalled her dream of the passionate scene in the studio and shifted slightly in her seat. "There has to be another connection, doesn't there?"

"Spirits don't always play by our rules, Natalie. We might never know the whole story."

Natalie refused to believe that. It was frustrating to only have pieces of the puzzle. "Could it be that I've finally admitted my own lesbianism?"

"That sounds logical, and that very well may be a connection. I've never seen you this comfortable or happy."

Natalie laughed. "I don't feel relaxed. I'm wound up tighter than a guitar string."

"Your spirit is happy, baby. It shows."

"Thank you, Mom." Natalie hugged her. "We better turn in."

Natalie said good night at her mother's door and went into her own room.

The window was wide open.

She had a momentary little shock then remembered she'd wished for the women to stay with her. As long as they rid the house of the dark man, she could live with the residual feminine energy.

Natalie took a shower before going to bed. When she saw her pretty new dress hanging on the door she recalled the scene in the dressing room. Mary was right, she thought. The seed was planted. She sat at her old-fashioned vanity and braided her wet hair. She tried to honestly appraise the woman looking back at her. Thirty-two wasn't old. Hell, these days fifty was the new thirty, right? Well, that practically made her a teenager!

Her image in the mirror seemed to shimmer and shift then Natalie was looking at her sixteen-year-old self. Red, angry acne appeared on cheeks that puffed up to resemble the chubby girl she'd been. She felt a sharp pain against her lips and instantly recalled the sensation of metal braces on her teeth. *No!* She wasn't that girl anymore and refused to let a snotty stranger push those buttons and make Natalie see this girl she was in the past.

Her reflection slowly returned to the present, which left her with the thought that Van might break her heart. Natalie had no idea where to put the hateful remarks she'd heard. Like a virus, the ugly words wanted to spread and create new insecurities. She had a hard time reconciling the way Van looked at her and made her feel with the different picture that spiteful woman created that afternoon.

God, was that only hours ago? It felt like days. Natalie went to her bed. Well, the seed may have been planted, but she didn't have to water it. She was future tripping about a long-term relationship and she hadn't even slept with Van yet.

Natalie was exhausted when she lay her head on the pillow. The emotional roller coaster she'd been on since she arrived was racing like a slideshow behind her eyes. The divorce and the move. The ghosts and dreams. The personal revelations and lifestyle change.

Van's face came to mind. She recalled the whispered promise and felt a spear of lust between her thighs. Good Lord, Natalie thought. How could I have ever accepted that I was frigid and broken? She let herself float to sleep with images of Van undressing her and making good on her threat to make her scream.

❖

Natalie looked into the darkness and saw an oil lamp burning at the end of the hall. Her stomach filled with dread.

"Beth!" a loud voice boomed out. "You little bitch. You can't hide from me forever. It will go much worse for you if you don't come out right now. *Beth*!"

Shit. Natalie crouched beside a wooden chest outside one of the bedrooms. There was nowhere else in sight to hide. She dared a quick glimpse and saw a large shadow looming on the stairway. Natalie frantically tried to figure out where she should go. Where the hell *could* you go when you were stuck in someone *else's* memory?

Natalie jerked when she heard glass breaking downstairs. She crawled on her hands and knees to the banister and peeked over the landing. A large hand descended on the back of her neck, snatching her like a small, helpless kitten.

"There you are! I told you not to hide from me. Obviously, you need me to teach you another lesson." He shook her. "When will you learn?"

Natalie looked into his face and immediately wished she hadn't. His eyes were flat black, the eyes of a predator. She could discern no emotion other than his volatile, insane anger. Each time he shook her, his dark hair hung forward in oily strands, and spittle flew out of his mouth. It was the face of a psychopath. She began to tremble violently when the sound of his evil laughter seemed to vibrate the walls and windows rattled in their frames.

The sound of feet running up the stairs registered in her terrified brain.

"Let her go, Richard!" Sarah screamed, holding her hands in fists at her sides.

"This is between me and my wife, Sarah. I told you, you have no business here." He throttled Natalie hard enough to rattle her teeth. "Go on, go away or I'm going to think you're jealous."

Natalie was frantic. It was so cold she could see her breath expelling in a cold steam.

"On second thought, little sister, it's been such a long time, come here." Richard leaned over and grabbed Sarah by her hair and dragged her and Natalie to the master bedroom. "You can watch." He giggled in a high-pitched voice.

Sarah screamed. She kicked and fought him as she struggled. Richard let go of her hair and shoved her hard, where she fell to the floor in front of the bed. He tossed Natalie onto the bed, and then backhanded Sarah when she tried to rise. Her head whipped around and hit the bedpost and she fell back again.

The windows were open and Natalie caught the familiar lavender scent in the breeze that blew in from outside. She scrambled to the top of the bed, willing herself to wake up. Richard's malevolent laughter echoed in her ears, leaving her terrified and paralyzed when she reached the headboard, panting like a cornered animal. She whimpered, horrified when he reached her. Richard wrapped one hand around her neck and smiled wickedly while he ripped at her nightgown with the other. Natalie gurgled as his grip tightened, cutting off her air completely. Please no, she thought. Not this. Her legs drummed on the bed and her vision dimmed.

From a faraway distance, Natalie heard an alarm going off then the noise abruptly stopped.

"Natalie? Honey, wake up." A gentle hand shook her shoulder.

Natalie gasped for a single breath and then took another.

"You're soaking wet," her mother said. "Are you okay?"

Natalie couldn't answer. She put her hand to her throat, still feeling the echo of Richard's vise grip. Her mother ran to the bathroom and came back with water. Natalie held the cold glass to her cheek. Her throat felt raw and her thighs burned. She decided not to tell her mother about the nightmare since she had to leave. She didn't want to worry her. She could have had the nightmare simply because they had learned so much about what happened here in the past. Her mind latched on to the explanation and refused to consider the alternative.

"I'm fine, Mom."

"You don't look fine."

"Just those scary stories last night, that's all."

Her mother looked doubtful. "Do you want me to stay?"

Natalie managed to smile weakly. "I'm good. Besides, Daddy needs you."

"Do you want to leave and come with me?"

Natalie considered it for a second. Nope, not running from anything. She shook her head. "I'm fine." She got out of the bed and winced inwardly. "I'll walk you out."

"Everything will be fine, Nat. I'll bring your father for a visit when he's walking better, okay?"

Natalie smiled at her. "That sounds wonderful."

They stood at the door and made their tearful good-byes. Natalie was going to miss her, having her mother around had made her feel safer. Natalie had no problem admitting to herself that she could see things others couldn't or wouldn't. She never thought too much about it until recently, but her gift had allowed her to become a pretty good judge of character in her teens. But over the last decade she must have repressed it. Otherwise, she would have had to take a closer look at her sham of a marriage and the denial she ruled her life with. It was a little disconcerting to have the ability come back to her as an adult.

Natalie went to the kitchen to brew some coffee. While she was waiting for it to brew, she made a to-do list. A strong feeling of *déjà vu* came over her. Had it only been just over a week since she sat here for the first time? She looked around her cheery kitchen and contemplated starting a fire in the hearth. Natalie wanted to keep busy so she wouldn't think about the brutal nightmare. The only thing she knew would keep out intruding thoughts was painting. She filled her cup and headed to the studio.

After she turned on every light and set up her easel, Natalie gathered her supplies. The silence was almost deafening and she felt a tiny chill when she realized the area was set up exactly as Beth had in her dream. The flashback brought memories of naked skin and incredible sensuality. Natalie was struck with inspiration, picked up her pencil, and began to sketch. Her focus narrowed to the paper in front of her and she let instinct guide her hand while the outside world ceased to exist.

CHAPTER TWELVE

Van escorted Natalie into the restaurant where she gave her name at the front desk. The patrons sat at intimate candlelit tables. This was definitely not the typical boardwalk crowd or the casual atmosphere of their first date. Van picked up the wine list. "Do you have a preference?"

Natalie smirked. "It depends on what we're eating."

Van felt heat from across the table. The double entendre washed over her. "Are we still talking about wine choices here?"

"Of course I'm talking about the wine. What else?"

Van saw the pink flush across Natalie's cheekbones and loved the shy, flirtatious behavior. She was completely different than her usually brazen companions. Van was just about to give her a list of *what else* when she was interrupted by a tall, blond, and apparently, very agitated woman. "Who the hell do you think you are, Easton? How come you never called?"

Shit. Van hesitated and quickly searched her memory while the woman crossed her arms over her chest and tapped her foot. Then she remembered. "Lynn?"

"Yes, Lynn," she spit out. When she opened her mouth again, Van abruptly excused herself from the table and, gripping her elbow, pulled Lynn out of the dining room to the hostess area.

Natalie felt drenched in ice water when she saw the triumphant look Lynn shot her over her shoulder. What was it with these tall and leggy fucking blondes, anyway? One stole her husband, okay, she admitted there was no great loss there, but this one stole her date right out from under her. Actually dismissed her as if she were nothing and no threat. Just like that woman had yesterday in the boutique. She had been willing to give Van the benefit of the doubt regarding her reputation until she showed her different. Two separate blondes in two days were a little much. Natalie stood and reached for her purse.

"Please don't go," Van said. "I'm sorry for that. I can explain."

Natalie stared at her standing there with her hands in her pockets. Every reasonable voice in her head was telling her to run. But it was her heart that saw Van and the utterly vulnerable expression on her face. It was Natalie's compassion that had her slowly lowering back into her chair. "What are we really doing here, Van?"

"Well, I'm hoping we are going to drink some good wine and have a nice dinner."

"You know what I mean." Natalie realized that while she had been an open book, the same wasn't true for Van. "I don't know much about you at all. Why is that?"

The waiter chose that moment to stop by. After he left, Van started to talk. "When I was twelve, my mother died. One minute she was fine and the next, she was gone." She snapped her fingers. "Just like that. Aneurism."

Natalie covered Van's hand with her own. "I'm so sorry. That must have been hard."

"It was. Dad did the best that he could. It couldn't have been easy for him, losing his wife, running a business, raising a daughter on the razor edge of puberty. It helped having so many aunts willing to step in. I was in high school when I discovered I was much more interested in what the cheerleaders were doing than the guys on the football field. I loved everything about girls. The way this one walked and that one smelled. How they laughed and that one was soft and this one was…" She trailed off.

"I get the point," Natalie interjected. "Go on."

"In college, I was a bit of a dog." Van grinned ruefully. "Then I met Cara." Van's voice broke a little. "And all the other women became invisible to me because she was everything, you know?"

Natalie didn't, but she wanted to. Oh, how she wanted to. What would it be like to be the recipient of all that emotion? To know that you put that look on someone's face of utter devotion? "Is Cara's picture the one at your father's house?"

Van nodded. "We were together for nearly eleven years before the cancer came and she died."

Natalie felt her eyes fill with sympathy when she heard the pain behind the explanation.

"The last six years have been a little blurry. I drank; I drank a lot. I didn't always know the names of the women I woke up next to, nor did I care to. I was empty."

That, Natalie could understand. She wanted to comfort Van and perhaps take the obvious hurt away, because it was in her nature to do so. But still, there was that small voice in her head that told her to wait until she could trust Van. The waiter took away their half-empty plates, and Natalie excused herself to the bathroom where she had an argument with herself. On one hand, she wanted Van so much it made her dizzy. On the other, and this was the biggie, she didn't want to be hurt again. She knew she would never be able to have a friends-with-benefits-type relationship; she wasn't built that way emotionally. If only she'd slept with her that first night, because now, she wanted more, much more.

She was torn. Natalie knew she already had feelings for her. But was that because of Van or because of her own new beliefs?

Would it be realistic that any woman she was attracted to would make her feel this way? No, she continued to argue. Otherwise, she would have known she was a lesbian, right?

Enough. It was all too much. Natalie patted cold water on her face. And until she answered these questions and sorted it out, she wouldn't be going home with Van. Natalie wanted her first time to be special. She would essentially be offering up her emotional virginity, and she wasn't going to give it to someone she didn't trust with her heart. She snapped her compact shut.

Van watched Natalie come out of the bathroom in her sexy blue dress and noticed the distant look on her face. For the first time, she was almost ashamed of the way she'd lived for the last six years.

She wanted to reassure her that she *was* different, but she knew the words would only sound empty. Had she really just bared her soul? Van never talked about Cara. Ever. She'd held herself aloof for so long she was unsure of how to act with someone she cared about.

Van held her hand out and Natalie took it as they walked out. Van was relieved that she didn't appear to have shut her completely out.

"I had a lovely time," Natalie said politely.

The remark startled a laugh out of Van. "You did not."

Natalie bumped her with her shoulder. "I got to know more about you."

"What? That I was loose?" Van felt nauseated.

"That you're loyal to those you love. That you had great losses in your life."

They stopped by the truck and Natalie put her arms around Van. "And that you're a slut puppy."

Van froze. Natalie tilted her head back and gave her a half smile. "But that doesn't necessarily change how I feel about you."

"How do you feel about me, Natalie?" Van was surprised to realize that she wanted to know, that it mattered so much to her.

Natalie didn't answer before she climbed in the truck. The ride home was silent and Van drove the distance and tried not to be nervous. "It's a beautiful house, Natalie."

"A beautiful *haunted* house."

"Do you really *like* the pink?" Van realized she was stalling, but she'd blurted the question before thinking.

Natalie laughed. "I hadn't thought about it, but the color does kind of look like Pepto-Bismol, doesn't it?"

When they reached her front door, Natalie leaned against it. "I love spending time with you. I've enjoyed every moment."

Van was worried this might be a kiss-off. "But?"

"But come here." Natalie drew herself up to whisper after Van leaned. "When we make love?"

"Uh, huh. When." Van felt a lump form in her throat.

"You're going to scream *my* name and you will *never* forget it."

The words went straight to Van's core. "Uh."

"Good night." Natalie walked into her house and shut the door.

Hot damn. Van felt thunderstruck and sat on the porch for a few seconds to make sure her legs would carry her back to her truck.

❖

Natalie changed her clothes and climbed the stairs to her studio. Her sketch hung on the wall behind the blank canvas. She felt pounded with sexual frustration; her muscles were tied in knots. She didn't much like the feeling, and for the first time since the divorce, she admitted that Jason may have had a point. If this is what he'd felt—this hollow ache—she could almost feel sorry for him. Just because she felt steadier now and she could somewhat understand his behavior, didn't mean that she forgave the betrayal. But she could perceive how it may have happened. It wasn't as personal as she previously thought. Then she dismissed him from her mind and recalled the scene on the porch.

The look on Van's face! The fact that she had unnerved her gave her a sense of pride, and a surge of sexual power rushed through Natalie. She put on her smock and looked for her palette to mix the paint she would need.

One drawer after another yielded nothing. They were gone. What the hell? She *knew* she'd unpacked them and put them in the cabinet. Natalie rubbed the chill on her arms. She refused to be afraid just as she knew she didn't want to think that something paranormal was going on.

She was pissed off and that was better than afraid any day of the week. "I'll just go and buy more paint tomorrow," she said to the empty room. Natalie tilted her head and listened, but after hearing nothing and no reply, she went to her room.

The window was closed. She sniffed the air but detected nothing but the trace of perfume she'd put on earlier in the evening before her date. This was good, she thought. Now she could convince herself that her supplies went missing *before* the house cleansing. She was truly without any spirits. Maybe she could get a dog. A little one that would shower her with love and her home wouldn't feel so empty.

She wouldn't feel so alone.

❖

Van shoved the receipts she had shuffled umpteen times to the side of her desk. She turned to the window and watched the rain fall.

God, she was confused. An image of Natalie underneath her, her long hair spread under and around her, had burned itself into her mind, and it was there every time she closed her eyes. Natalie had snuck around her defenses and knocked her flat on her ass right in the middle of a guilty puddle of uncertainty.

Every door she shut with a woman behind it in the last six years echoed in her mind. And the one that had been closed tightly for a very long time was unlocking. Talking about Cara last night turned the key.

Cara.

Van had just turned twenty-two and she and the rest of the softball team were celebrating their fifteen-run win at Lanie McCrath's house. Groups formed on the front lawn and loud rock music spilled out the open doors and windows.

Annette was sitting next to her on the stone wall in the backyard and they were arguing good-naturedly about who could have what girl in attendance and whether they were gay or straight. They were everywhere that night, tall women, short women, voluptuous and thin. Blondes, brunettes, redheads, and everything in between, Van loved them all. Her androgynous beauty almost always guaranteed she never slept alone.

Van spotted a couple of sporty femme types sitting on the couch inside and stood to get a better look inside the glass door. They were from the opposing team they had just whupped and she told herself she should just go in and make them feel better for losing. After all, they still had a chance to score. She grinned and felt terribly clever for thinking of the line, then started to approach them.

"Leaving me for a blonde, Easton?"

"Absolutely, Chapowitz."

Annette smiled and waved her on. "I'm sure I can find a big bad butch to take me home. Especially since I'm still wearing my shorts" She waved a hand over her shapely legs and indicated the uniform she was still wearing. "Go play." Annette stood to walk toward another promising group of women.

"Wait." Van grabbed her arm. There, by the sliding doors, was a tall girl with long dark hair she had never seen before. She was talking, and perfect white teeth glowed against the amber color of her skin. Her full breasts were outlined by a little white tank top that showed a strip of tanned stomach and the flash of a rhinestone piercing. Lips that were painted red pursed to kiss the cheek of the girl she was talking to.

Van's heart stopped and she felt as if a hand clenched her stomach in a tight fist. Her world narrowed to a single glance that held this woman's beauty in its center. "Who is that?" She pulled her gaze away to look to Annette for an answer.

"That, my friend, is Cara Martinez. New student, transferred from the East Coast. Would you like to meet her?"

Yes, she would, and they had been inseparable for ten years.

Van looked inside herself and found the places in her heart that had been filled with Cara and discovered they weren't empty after all. There was a small pilot light burning, and the accelerant was a small, bubbly redhead.

Lust was something she could deal with very well and had over the last few years. She never went out of her way; women were just naturally drawn to her. What she couldn't figure out today was why *this* woman and not any of *those* women?

Who was she kidding? This thing with Natalie *meant* something. She dialed her number. Van's stomach was in anxious knots and she rubbed it absentmindedly when she got the busy signal. She tried three more times with the same result.

The cell phone subscriber you are trying to reach is not accepting calls at this time...

She tried the house phone again and it was still busy. Van realized she was being obsessive and tried to get a handle on it. She could go to the greenhouse and help, or work on a new fountain, something, to get her mind off Natalie.

Or she could drive up to her house. There was a work crew there. Natalie didn't have to know that Van didn't normally work with the initial clean up crew.

She wrote a note to her father, grabbed her truck keys, and went out the side door. When she arrived at Natalie's house, Van took in the work being done. Mowers kicked clouds of dirt and loose debris as they pushed and jumped over the uneven terrain of the yard. Progress was slow, but the possibilities were beginning to show beneath the loose earth.

Van parked in the empty driveway in front of the garage. Natalie didn't appear to be home. She felt some of her anxiety lessen. When she got out, she spotted the envelope on the front door with her name on it.

Inside was a key to the back door and a short note that Natalie wouldn't be back until later in the afternoon. She was running into the city for painting supplies, but Van and her crew were welcome to use the restroom and help themselves to water or soda that was in the refrigerator.

Van was disappointed she wasn't home but relieved that the note was friendly. Van couldn't ever remember the last time she'd been insecure about anything. She mentally shook herself. This was ridiculous, this emotional ride she was on. She spotted Rick and he waved her over. That was better, she thought. Work was always a welcome distraction.

Van cut, dug, and marked out boundaries for the new landscaping design. She hardly noticed when the equipment became quiet but was aware when various trucks started and left. She glanced at her watch and was surprised to see that two hours had flown by. She crossed to where Rick was standing. "What's going on?"

"The guys are taking a break and going somewhere to use the bathroom and grab something to eat. What can I get you?"

"What do you mean use the bathroom? I left the back door open so you all could use the downstairs one."

"No offense, Van. None of the guys want to go into the house. It's, well, you know." He sheepishly looked at her. "So what can I get you?"

"Are you fucking kidding me?" One look at his face told her he wasn't. She started to ask but just shook her head. "Just get me whatever you're having. Thanks."

Van brushed the dirt off her hands and headed toward the back door. She would show these superstitious *boys* that there was nothing to be afraid of. She walked through the kitchen to the downstairs bathroom and shut the door. She had to admit though, her father's story made her see the house in a new light. The old stories had a little more credence. But Natalie hadn't talked about ghosts at all last night on their date.

When she was busy washing her hands, solid, heavy footsteps echoed from the second floor over Van's head. She turned the water off so she could hear. Maybe she had been mistaken. Nope, there they were again, muffled through the ceiling.

Van was pissed. None of her crew had permission to be on the second floor, especially not exploring. She would fire the offender on the spot. "Who's there?" she yelled.

No answer. She stood still for a moment. Nothing. Van climbed the stairs cautiously, hoping to catch the intruder. Icy fingers started tap dancing on her spine and the hair stood on the back of her neck. She froze when she heard a voice whisper.

"*Get out.*"

A door in the hallway behind her slammed shut, reverberating through the stillness like a gunshot.

Van turned slowly and tried to breathe past the lump in her throat. It was one thing to hear a story about ghosts and believe in spirits—in theory. But never having a personal experience before, she wasn't prepared to deal with one.

Sunlight poured into the hallway from what appeared to be a guest room, but it did little to dispel the chill in the air. Van went to the master bedroom and tried to dismiss the whisper. She convinced herself that it was one of the guys messing with her. She was going to kick some major ass.

With the sound of her own ragged breathing in her ear, she inched her hand to the doorknob. Natalie's bed was neatly made and the curtains open to the sunshine. She quickly searched the room and adjoining bathroom. Van backed out of the room and after a moment of apprehension, she closed the door behind her.

No one was hiding upstairs. Van felt a little foolish but still had to force herself from running back outside. The last thing she was going to do was make an ass out of herself in front of the crew.

Rick met her at the back door. "There's been an accident."

❖

After she left the emergency room, she told the crew to take the rest of the day off. Van hadn't wanted to give them any more time to grumble about ghosts. She'd called her father earlier so he could fill out the proper forms for the company. One of the laborers had been working in the side yard clearing out brush when an object flew up under the mower and hit him in the head. Six hours and ten stitches later, he was sent home with some gnarly painkillers and instructions to rest for a few days.

The flying object was currently in the bed of her truck. Once she had brushed the dirt off of it, she saw that it was a beautiful old hairbrush, solid silver with a delicate etching of roses budding on a vine that wrapped around the solid handle. It was in excellent condition and Van saved it, along with a small traveling case found buried near the south wall of the house, to return to Natalie.

Van took a critical look at her own yard. Her grass was looking a little ragged around the edges and her flowers needed some attention. She had a reputation to uphold and she didn't want to be like the proverbial carpenter whose house was never done or the mechanic who had four clunkers sitting in his yard.

Van spent the next couple of hours in her element, happily cutting, trimming, and deadheading various plants. After the lawn was mowed, she sat on her front porch and sipped a cold soda. Van closed her eyes to let the afternoon sun warm her face. As she relaxed, Natalie's smiling face came to mind. It felt good to sit here and just be in the moment. She didn't feel as if she was running away from anything. For the first time in many years, she was thinking of running to someone and she was filled with a sense of happy anticipation.

Perhaps she might fulfill the promise she'd made to Cara so long ago.

❖

Natalie parked her car in the driveway. The sun was setting and turned the windows in the front of the house blood red. She stared through the windshield, grateful to find the window closed as she left it.

She was delighted to find the colossal mess in the front of the house. Any normal person would see chaos, she thought. She was pleased with the progress and could see the amazing potential. She was tickled pink. Like her house. She giggled, amused by the thought.

The day in the city rejuvenated her. Natalie had stopped in her favorite salon and got her hair trimmed then spent happy hours in the art supply warehouse putting a major ding in her credit card. After lunch, she sat and people watched.

Natalie studied every attractive woman that she spotted and tried imagining getting naked with them. Every time she attempted, each woman became Van. Well, that answered one of her questions. It *was* Van she wanted.

On the drive home, Natalie decided she would go with her impulses and quit living in her head. If there was any negative aftermath for being impulsive she would simply deal with it later. She was done hiding and pretending.

She felt lighter when she opened the trunk to retrieve her bags. Natalie quickly realized that she would have to make two trips. Had she really bought that much? She dropped the purchases in front of the staircase and went to the kitchen.

A note lay on the table from Van.

Natalie, tried calling you several times. Please get a hold of me when you get back. I would love to see you. Van.

Natalie was puzzled and dug in her purse to find her phone. The only person that called her that day was the manager at the art gallery. Her previous works were sold out, and he asked if she could provide a few more in time for their show in the early fall as they still needed to stretch and frame the large canvasses.

She checked the call log but didn't see any from Van. Weird. The answering machine light wasn't blinking either.

Natalie jumped when the wall extension rang loudly in the quiet kitchen.

"Hello?"

She heard nothing but static on the line. "Hello?"

The sound of heavy breathing filled her ear and she slammed the receiver. The phone immediately rang again.

"Hello?"

Natalie got chills when guttural laughter erupted. She was immediately aware of dark energy emanating from the sound and hung up again.

Her cell phone sang on the table. Okay, this was scary. "*What do you want*?" she screamed.

"Um, Natalie, is that you?"

"Van? Oh, God." She laughed nervously and ran a hand through her hair. "I'm so sorry. I thought you were a crank caller."

There was a pause. "Get many of those do you?"

"Just lately. How was your day?"

"Better now that I've finally got a hold of you. I thought you were trying to avoid me."

"I saw your note."

"Every time I tried to call your cell, it wasn't accepting calls. When I tried to call your house, it was always busy."

"For some reason, they didn't even register." Natalie was still spooked.

A door slammed upstairs and echoed in the kitchen. Natalie's thoughts sprinted. *Let me see, choice here. Home alone with a ghost or in bed with a beauty.*

She closed her eyes briefly. *Duh.* "Van? Do you want to go out tonight?"

CHAPTER THIRTEEN

Van came around the bend in the driveway and found Natalie waiting on the front porch. She had barely put the truck in park before she surprised her and jumped into the cab. "Let's go to your place."

Van stared at her. Where was shy Natalie? This one had her pinned to the seat with a smoldering look that was so hot; Van instantly felt heat between her thighs.

"Okay," she said simply before throwing the truck into reverse and speeding back the way she came.

Van hesitated before she pulled into the garage. "Last chance, Natalie. Are you sure about this? Because once I start, I'm going to really, really want to finish."

Natalie unbuckled her seat belt and threw herself to the driver's side. She held Van's face in her hands and looked straight into her eyes. "I have never wanted anyone as much as I want you right now."

Van growled deep in her throat.

"Omigod, Van. Now. Get out of the truck, now."

Van pulled into the garage, opened her door, and reached to pull Natalie out of the driver's side. They had barely made it into the kitchen before Van picked her up and Natalie wrapped her legs around her. Van staggered to the counter to sit her on it.

Natalie grabbed her collar and kissed her breathless. Van didn't hold anything back; she threw herself into the kiss, barely letting either of them even catch a breath.

Wait. Van pulled back. "Stay here for a second."

"What?"

"I'll be right back." Van left Natalie on the counter and raced to her bedroom where she lit several candles and turned down the comforter. She was nervous about being Natalie's first, which unsettled her. She'd never had that responsibility before and it shook her confidence a little. She turned and saw Natalie standing in the doorway, looking stunning and fragile at the same time. The flickering candlelight reflected like flames off her hair. She walked toward Van and pulled the pins out of the mass of hair until it tumbled around her shoulders.

Van traced her hands down Natalie's back and entangled them in her hair. She pulled her away from her chest so she could look at her. "You are so beautiful," she whispered as she lowered her head to kiss her. The heat that bubbled below Natalie's innocence took her breath away as she tenderly probed Natalie's lips with her tongue. She felt the impact of Natalie's soft sigh of submission charge her skin. Urgency made her lift Natalie onto the bed and her hair fanned out beneath her. Her eyes, oh God, her radiant eyes held unfathomable depth and traces of unspoken promises. It was the image already burned into Van's mind, made real in one glorious moment.

Natalie was shocked at her own behavior. For someone who avoided sex as a rule, this aching need to be with Van threw all her inhibitions right out the nearest window. There would be no pretense, no guile, just a mutually driving force to sate their desire for each other. She reached up to unlace her dress at the collar. She laughed when Van did that sexy growl and moved her hands out of the way. "God, I love that," she said. "Do it again."

Van's voice thickened. "You like that?"

Natalie arched her back in response when Van growled for her again. Van pinned her wrists to the bed and bit the top of the lace tie, pulling the bow out with her teeth. When she felt Van's hands cover her naked breast she heard whimpering. She was stunned to discover it was coming from her own throat. She put a hand out to Van's shoulder so she could sit and finish unlacing her dress then pull it off. She reached up for Van's shirt and unbuttoned it with shaky hands. Natalie's heart raced as she watched Van slip the shirt off and unhook her bra to throw it behind her. Her mouth went dry at the sight of Van peeling off her jeans to stand naked at the edge of the bed.

Natalie shyly touched her palm to Van's stomach and felt the hard muscles jump at the contact. She brought her other hand over to trace Van's hip. When she heard Van sigh she felt an answering tug in her own stomach and her body felt heavy. Then she felt herself being guided onto her back. She registered the flickering candles and the sound of her own heavy breathing before time no longer existed. This moment, right here, right now became her world.

Natalie felt Van's breasts brush her stomach as she lowered herself gently onto her. She jumped with electrical desire and pulled Van closer to feel naked flesh alongside her own. She nipped Van's lip and was rewarded with another growl. Pressure was building in her body, and she felt a sense of urgency that almost scared her.

Natalie melted when Van's hand began stroking her gently, first circling her neck and then down her sides, lightly raking her nails along her inner thighs. Liquid fire rushed to her center and they shared hot, tandem breaths. Van's eyes stayed open and focused on her own. Natalie's fingers clawed into the mattress when she felt Van's teeth bite her nipples in turn then she trailed kisses down her stomach. Van's knee pressed insistently between her thighs until Natalie realized she wanted her to spread them. She let her knees fall open and Van mounted her, pinning her with her pelvis and moving in tiny circles. Natalie strained against her, bucking her hips. Van's soft skin sliding against her own was a whisper of ecstasy filled with a heat she had never felt. "Please, Van." She dug her nails into Van's back and hid her face against Van's long neck.

"Sssh. Baby, it's okay. I've got you." Van reached between their bodies, her fingers probing gently for Natalie's clitoris. "God, you are hot, so incredibly wet. Is this for me?" Van leaned up on her elbow to look at Natalie's face.

"Yes." Wave after wave of emotion assaulted her, leaving her trembling, as vulnerable as she was naked. Her orgasm ripped through her and her body arched into Van's. The pleasure was almost too intense. It didn't plateau; it kept rising until Natalie closed her eyes and trembled with aftershocks.

Natalie finally opened her eyes and turned her head to gaze at Van. The disappointment and acute shame she usually experienced the proverbial morning after was glaringly absent. Sex with Van had been a miracle. The part of Natalie's brain that criticized was blessedly silent.

Van looked concerned. "What's wrong, sweetheart?"

"That was incredible, you know? Is it always like this?"

"Always like what? Mind-blowing? Magnificent?" Van gave her a slow smile, teasing her. "Did you see fireworks?"

"Van, I think I saw God." Natalie chuckled and sat with her legs crossed, pulling the sheet to her waist, leaving her breasts bare. It's like I've been ordering pizza my entire life when what I really wanted was Chinese food."

Van laughed and stroked her sides gently. "But the pizza man kept telling you that you loved his pizza, right?"

Natalie nodded. "I knew that I really didn't like it. For some reason, this"—she waved her arms over the completely disheveled bed—"this didn't occur to me." Natalie felt the tears threaten behind her eyes. "How could I not know about this?"

"How about because you always did what was expected of you?"

Natalie rose on her knees and straddled Van's hips.

Van grinned wickedly at her. "What are you doing?"

"I'm making a memory of this most important moment of my life." She lightly caressed Van's breasts, elated that her nipples instantly went hard. "I can't believe how amazing this feels." Natalie softly traced Van's lips and jumped when her finger disappeared into her hot mouth. She gasped, instantly drenching Van's thighs. "Oh. My. God."

"There you go again. No, sweetheart, it's just me." Van flipped Natalie onto her back and kissed her long and hard. When she was gasping for breath, she whispered in her ear. "So, wanna go to heaven again?" She smothered Natalie's giggles with a deep kiss.

❖

"Do you have to go to work?" Natalie asked.

"Yes. There's a big shipment coming in from one of our main suppliers at noon and I have to be there to inspect it. My father doesn't want to be bothered with that aspect of the business anymore. He just wants to sit outside on one of the rockers and shoot the breeze with the customers." Van watched a thought cross Natalie's expressive face and thought she knew what she was thinking. On many levels that she didn't want to explore yet, Van knew Natalie wasn't a one-night stand for her. She thought of all the lines she could spit out and make Natalie feel better. Words that she could give to anyone else without even blinking twice. But the reassurances stuck in her throat.

The awkward silence stretched out between them until Natalie broke it, clearly trying to ease the tension. "Where are my panties?"

Van laughed and slapped her lightly on the ass, relieved for the moment. "They're in my scrapbook, where else?"

"Seriously, Van." She ruffled the covers. "A-ha! I found them" Natalie stood and fell back on the bed. "Wow. I am pleasantly sore in places that I didn't even know I had."

Van smiled at her. "That's a good thing, sweetheart."

Natalie cupped her hand on Van's cheek. "I'm overwhelmed, and I don't know how to articulate it yet. But I don't know what the rules are here. Morning afters always felt shameful and uncomfortable. This is completely new territory for me and I don't want to get lost. This has been the single most amazing experience of my life, but I don't know where we go from here. I'm all wrapped up in you and I'm terrified."

Van had a few of those same thoughts as well this morning but preferred to shut them down until she could think about how she felt. Natalie humbled her this morning. "Better to be terrified of the ghosts in your house than me."

"Did you have to go there?" Natalie asked.

"What happened yesterday?"

"You didn't give me a chance to tell you earlier." Natalie smiled and flexed her long fingers. "I'm an artist. I have selective memory, and I can be temperamental and downright eccentric."

Van was amused. "It's part of your charm, right?"

"Damn straight." Natalie said and reached for her dress to head into the bathroom.

"Natalie?" Van asked. She looked like a goddess standing there in her skimpy panties, tumbled hair, and wearing a blush on top of it all.

"Yes?"

"Brace yourself." Van smoothly launched herself, tackling Natalie back onto the bed. "I am the boss and I can be late."

❖

After a red-hot kiss at the door and a promise to call later, Van dropped Natalie off and left for the nursery. With Van out of physical proximity, Natalie could think about the major turn her life had taken.

Flashbacks came to her in an intense rush. She thought of soft breasts and hot skin that felt like velvet over solid muscles. Natalie smiled. Everything had felt so natural. There were no awkward moments, at least until they had to part. Of course she was a bit shy and uncertain, but only because she hadn't ever been made love to before, not like that. How could she put into words the way colors bled into her consciousness and splashed over all the shades of gray she had lived with for so many years? The passion she had only previously had a hint of when painting flooded her senses until all she could *do* was feel? How terrifying and satisfying it was all at the same time.

Natalie felt gloriously alive while she took her shower. She couldn't help but smile while she thought *this* is what well-loved felt like. The depth of satisfaction made her want to purr. Natalie dried her body tenderly. There was not an inch of her that wasn't kissed, caressed, or nibbled on. She hung up her towel and turned to the mirror then saw the new message written in the steam.

Run!

"The hell I will," she said in an even tone, even as she was royally mad for the intrusion. She marched to her dresser to pull on comfortable clothes then went to her studio.

The completed sketch on the wall begged her attention. Though she desperately wanted to paint Sarah and Beth entwined on the chaise, she had the gallery obligation to fulfill.

Natalie propped two of the promised three paintings against the wall so she could create another to complement them. She crouched in front of the canvas women, her bottom lip caught between her teeth.

The Winter Queen on her throne of ice stared back at her. She touched the woman's mouth and wondered if she'd been thinking of how it would feel to kiss those full red lips in the back of some recess in her mind when she created her.

Frigid. Jason's voice whispered in her memory.

The word intruded, but Natalie smiled. The ugly label no longer had any power over her. She turned to the Fire Empress standing defiantly in front of her throne. Flames licked the hem of her gown and piercing eyes dominated her face. Her long hair blew around her, filling the canvas. She almost seemed to be inviting someone to come get burned while at the same time her expression said she knew that no one would dare.

Had she painted this one to represent her buried passion? It certainly seemed so. Yes, the signs were here in her art. Her dream lovers and hidden selves. Natalie felt fresh pride in her work, looking at it with clear eyes.

The next in the series would be Earth Mother. Natalie assembled her new supplies, faced the empty canvas, took a deep breath, and systematically closed out distractions—the landscaping crew, her thoughts, the ticking of the clock in the corner. An idea formed. And then reformed.

Natalie picked up her brush and began creating.

Some hours later, she became aware again and set her brush down. Natalie looked out the window and saw dark storm clouds rolling and gathering in the evening dusk. She rubbed her aching shoulder and turned to look at what she'd nearly completed. In an instant, her breath left her lungs in a rush and she dropped to her knees.

Natalie had painted herself. No, not her—Beth's gaunt face stared out at her, a horrific purple and yellow bruise covered the left side of her face and her bottom lip was bloody and swollen. Natalie gasped and reached up to touch her own face and watched, terrified, as Beth mirrored her movement.

Tears were falling down her battered face and she appeared to be trying to speak. Rain pelted the windows and Natalie realized it was herself making the wounded noises in her own throat. She backed up to the wall in a sitting fetal position and rubbed her eyes.

"*Help us!*"

"I can't help you!" Natalie cried out. "I don't know how!"

"*Find the key!*"

The door at the bottom of the stairs slammed shut. Terror raced through Natalie's bloodstream, churning her stomach, and she broke out in a cold sweat. She willed herself to wake up, to believe that this wasn't real.

The door slammed again and Natalie thought her heart might burst. More thunder shook the house and the lights went out. One of the front windows shattered; the curtains blew in with the force of the wind, rain soaking everything in its path.

Loud footsteps sounded on the stairs. Her throat clenched and Natalie couldn't breathe. Deep, masculine laughter boomed and echoed around the dark room.

Natalie screamed. "Go away, you're not *real!*"

Beth cried out. "*The key!*"

The easel moved with unseen force and flew at Natalie's head.

Van stood at the front door and shook the rain from her hair. What was taking Natalie so long to answer? Her car was out front.

Was someone crying? One moment she could hear it and the next, the sound was swept away by the wind. Van left the porch to check out the front windows. There were lights on in the third floor turret.

Natalie screamed and adrenaline flooded Van's veins. She ran around to the back to use her key and raced through the house then pounded up the stairs. It was quiet now. Too quiet. Van was dimly aware of a pressure on her chest when she tried to open the door to the studio. It was stuck. She wanted to smash through it, but the door opened outward.

Thc knob finally turned and she flew up the stairs. When she saw Natalie on the floor she ran to her. She was struggling for breath and Van could see her rapid pulse pounding in her neck.

Van was alarmed at how cold she was. "Natalie?" She patted her face. "Baby, wake up." When she didn't get any reaction, she shook harder. "Come on, come back to me."

"Van?" she whispered. "Be careful of the glass."

"What glass?"

Natalie gained her feet and tried to drag Van to the stairs. "We have to hide. He's here!"

Van used force to still her. "Sweetheart, there's no one here."

Natalie looked around with wide eyes. Everything looked normal. The window was closed and in one piece; the easel was still set up where she placed it. "It was so real."

"What happened, Natalie?" Van led her to the chair and sat her down.

Natalie told her about the painting and apparent shift of reality.

Van believed her. How could she not after hearing everything that happened in this house? "What key?"

Natalie's color looked better. "I have no idea."

"Have you eaten today?"

"No, I was up here painting for hours." Natalie finally stood and walked over to the canvas then cried out in shock.

Van rushed over to see what she was seeing.

The canvas was completely white.

❖

Natalie tried to call her mother. "Damn it. Nothing but static."

"Here, try mine."

"No signal." Natalie went to the refrigerator and started to pull together a fruit and cheese tray. "Grab me some crackers out of the pantry, could you please?" She still felt a little shaky, but refused to give in to the fear.

"Do you want to go to my place?"

She looked over at Van and noticed how pale she was. "God, I'm sorry. I never thought how this might be affecting you; how insane I must seem."

"It *is* a little surreal." Van popped a grape into her mouth. "When I was using the restroom earlier, I thought I heard somebody walking upstairs and I could almost swear I heard somebody tell me to get out. You have to admit it's a little scary. Okay, it's a lot scary."

"I wouldn't blame you if you wanted to leave," Natalie said. "I would understand." So much for her budding romance, she thought sadly.

"Don't you want to after that scene upstairs?" Van pointed to the ceiling. "Aren't you afraid at all?"

"I'd be lying if I said I wasn't." The chilling memory of the—what should she call it, vision—was fading, but Natalie's heart still felt wounded. The pain she felt was real, even if it wasn't actually hers.

Van's voice interrupted her thoughts. "Do *you* want to leave?"

Natalie thought of how many times she'd bowed to someone else's expectations and did exactly what they thought she should. Her fear was replaced with defiance. The only victims here, as she saw it, were Beth and Sarah. "No, I want to stay and help them." Her voice came out as strong as she suddenly felt.

"How?"

"I have to find the key."

"Okay, where do we start?"

Natalie felt her heart skip a beat; she said "we." It appeared that Van wasn't going to run screaming into the night. "I'm guessing we have to solve the mystery."

"Shouldn't we call in a paranormal team or something?"

The question amused Natalie. "My mother just left the other day. For most of my life, I accepted strange occurrences that didn't necessarily have any logical explanation, things that others aren't comfortable with. I got used to keeping most of it to myself for so long, I shut out *my* gift." This is another reason why, Natalie thought, she'd stayed in her sham of a marriage so long. Once you started building a brick wall of denial, it became easy to hide all sorts of things behind it.

"Okay," Van said. "Let's run this all down from the beginning."

Natalie began her story at the point she drove away from her old house.

Van listened while she wrote a bullet list. The whole thing was beginning to sound like a Hollywood script, except it was coming from Natalie, and she had a part in the movie. Everything that happened sounded irrational, but after having her own experience in the house, Van couldn't help but feel the story was plausible.

"This all fits in with what my dad said at dinner," she said when Natalie finished. "So the previous owners were only haunted by who they called the dark man, and we know as Richard."

Natalie nodded. "The asshole bully."

Van grinned; she couldn't help but think it was cute, hearing Natalie swear with that sweet voice of hers. "Back to the list. When *you* moved in, you dreamt of Sarah, who appeared to have thought you were Beth, who was married to the asshole bully, who also happened to be Sarah's brother."

"Pretty much, that's how I see it," Natalie said.

"And…" Van looked at her list. "You realized you were a lesbian during the course of the initial dreams."

"In the beginning, I think the dreams made some kind of connection. But I was sure when I met you."

"This brings us to my first connection, an ancestor who worked on this property." Van drew an arrow from her name to Natalie's on her paper. "The second connection I see is us together as a couple."

The basement door rattled in its frame and the hair rose on the back of Van's neck. "Jesus Christ, Natalie. A sane woman would run."

"Apparently, we pissed somebody off."

Van made eye contact with Natalie. She was already far more attached to her than she ever thought she would be when she met her. She loved that she looked fierce and not afraid. "Doesn't this feel a little pre-ordained to you?" Van didn't know how to feel about that at the moment, that someone or something else could plot her destiny.

Natalie looked thoughtful. "Because of the fact that I am the spitting image of Beth? Which, by the way, kind of gives me the willies, or because Beth moved in here and fell in love with Sarah?"

Van drew one more arrow. "Looks like both."

"Then I have to dig deeper to find more connections and the key."

A cool breeze blew through the kitchen. "Do you smell lavender?" Van asked.

Natalie nodded. "I'm going to take that as Beth and Sarah's agreeing with us *and* I'm not giving Richard a fucking inch."

"You're becoming quite the potty mouth."

Natalie blushed and started to say something, but Van interrupted her. "No, it's okay. I like it." Natalie had many facets and she found them all interesting. Life may have been much simpler before she met her, but it sure as hell wasn't as fascinating. She raised her water glass. "Here's to not giving Richard a fucking inch." She was done with the frightful portion of the evening's program.

"Let's go back to the part about you being certain of being a lesbian." Van stood and beckoned Natalie closer. "C'mere and show me." She opened her arms and held her tight before tipping her head for a kiss. Her mouth had barely touched Natalie's when the front door slammed, rattling the stained glass panels in their frames. Van startled and drew blood when she accidently nipped Natalie's lower lip. "I'm sorry, " she said. "That door was locked when I got here."

"Welcome to Natalie Land," she said solemnly. "All spooky, all the time."

"Where were we? Oh yes..." She spun Natalie around and nuzzled her neck. "You smell good."

Natalie sighed against her cheek. "So, Van, you want to see my etchings?"

"Oh yeah." Van followed her up the stairs.

Natalie ran outside into the dark night and pouring rain. Frantically, she looked around the overgrown yard and tried to place where the fountain should be. Thorns scraped and tore at her flesh as she pulled out brush with her bare hands. Her legs caught in the blackberry vines and she fell but did not stop tearing at the wall of weeds in front of her. *It's here, I know it. Please, I have to find it.* She pushed back her wet hair and pulled the last branch out of her way. She'd found the fountain. The once beautiful structure was now broken, the cherub missing from his perch. There was no cheerful bubbling; the water was dark, murky, and full of dead things. Natalie fell to her knees before the wreckage and bowed her head. Thunder rolled across the sky and a crack of lightning flashed overhead and startled Natalie into a rocking motion on her knees. Heart wrenching pain churned through her, and she cried in the dark. *What was she looking for?*

"Oh, honey, what happened to you?" Van dropped to her knees beside her.

Natalie looked at her and held out her hands, noticing blood for the first time. Dirt crusted under her fingernails and she was covered with nicks and scratches. "I found the fountain." Her throat felt scratchy and hoarse. She pointed to the crumbling structure just visible under a mountain of weeds, brush, and blackberry vines. She must have dug it out when she was…what? Sleepwalking? Her hands burned and she couldn't seem to stop crying.

"Come on. Let's get you to the house, okay?" Strong arms lifted her from the mud.

Van's eyes locked with Natalie's, the steady gaze making it easier for Natalie to pull herself together. Her knees threatened to give out, but Van held her steady through the house and back to the bedroom.

In the bright bathroom light, Natalie winced at her reflection. Her eyes looked too large for her face and several scratches welted her skin. Natalie limped to the edge of the tub while Van rubbed her down with a thick towel and then started picking sticks and brambles out of Natalie's wet and tangled hair.

This had to be the breaking point, Natalie thought. This is where Van would run. Hell, she wanted to run herself. Van held her chin gently and wiped her face.

"I woke up and you were gone."

"How did you know I was outside?"

"I heard someone crying."

Natalie considered the location she had found her. "But how could you have heard me from here? It's a long ways back and it's pouring rain outside."

"I repeat, I heard crying."

"I don't remember going outside. God, I don't even recall falling asleep." The last thing Natalie remembered was being completely sated and entwined with Van, inhaling her scent while she contentedly stroked the arm that held her. "Ouch!"

"I'm sorry," Van said. "Sit still. I have a few more to pull out. I think you're going to need a bath to clean out the scratches so I can see what I'm doing here."

"You act as if you find naked and muddy women outside in the rain every night of the week."

"Nope you're the first."

Natalie thought this must be the most bizarre night of her life. She was flirting and falling for Van while having the worst nightmares she'd ever experienced. The severe contradiction of emotion was leaving her a little hysterical around the edges and she was having a hard time processing the opposing feelings. She took a couple of deep breaths. She could do this; just one step at a time was all that was required.

"Have you ever walked in your sleep before?"

Natalie shook her head then shivered. "It's a little fuzzy, but I remember seeing Richard ripping something from Beth's neck and throwing it out the window."

"Did you see what it was?"

Natalie tried to focus but couldn't quite grasp the details. "No, I just knew it was imperative that I find what was hidden out there. I was consumed with grief, like someone I loved had died."

Van looked away and Natalie realized what she had said. "I'm so sorry." One more ghost for her to deal with.

"It's okay. I know the feeling. Let's get the tub filled." Natalie and Van went into the large shower to rinse off with the handheld attachment while the bathtub filled. When Natalie opened the door, she darted a glance to the mirror to see if there were any messages and was relieved when she saw none.

She crossed to sit back on the ledge and Van knelt between her legs, resting her forehead against hers. Natalie felt Van's rapid pulse in their joined hands. "I'm sorry, Van. I feel stupid about this whole thing."

"Hush. Let me hold you for a minute. You were gone and I heard crying. I think my heart stopped for a second when I saw the front door standing open." Van brought Natalie's hand to her lips and kissed her scratches gently. "Honey, if you wanted the yard done tonight, you could have just asked."

And there it was, Natalie thought, her reassurance that she hadn't scared Van away. Not yet, anyway. She laughed softly, grateful for the olive branch. "I think next time, I just might," she said as she slipped into the water. "Oh God, that burns. I have scratches everywhere."

"And I'm going to kiss every one of them."

Natalie flashed on Van's excellent kisses then admired the way her biceps flexed when she reached for the soap and washcloth to make lather while Natalie picked the last of the sticks out of her hair.

"Lay back."

Natalie ducked under. When she surfaced she lay back on the seat, lifting a leg to check for wounds. Van held her calf and washed her feet.

"They aren't as bad as I thought. Give me the other one now."

Natalie braced on her elbows with both legs in the air. Van used small, circular motions to travel higher on her thighs. The sensation was incredibly hypnotic and Natalie sighed softly, opening her knees to give Van more access to continue the caresses. Her eyes closed and she willed Van to reach the flesh that quivered in anticipation of her touch.

The phone rang in the bedroom, startling Natalie into sitting.

"Who is that at this time of night?" Van asked.

Natalie felt heavy with desire but tried to pull herself out of her sexual haze. "It's my mother."

❖

The sun was just rising when Van crept into the bathroom to get dressed. She had just enough time to go home and shower before she should be at work. She hunkered beside Natalie and kissed her gently, so as not to wake her. They had stayed up even later after Natalie's mother suggested they burn more sage and white candles. Even so, she had serious misgivings about leaving her alone.

"Morning," Natalie said sleepily. "Running off on me?"

"No. I just wanted to kiss your pretty face before I have to go to work."

"It's Saturday."

"Best day of the week for us." She pulled a strand of hair out of Natalie's eyes. "Do you want me to stay?"

"I'll be fine." Natalie looked at the clock and groaned before she slid back under the covers. "I'm going to go back to sleep for a while."

"Are you sure?"

"Van, I'll be fine. Go."

"Are artists always so grumpy in the morning?"

"Only the really good, creative ones, bye now."

Van kissed her again, lingering. She didn't want to leave, but her father depended on her. She kissed Natalie's bandaged hands and backed out of the room. The hallway still held traces of the sage burned only a short time ago.

It reminded Van that there was something to guard against. The unexplained events she'd experienced had left her a little numb, a little disoriented. And, she could admit to herself, a little afraid and uneasy. Sunlight streamed in the stained glass windows, reflecting a happy rainbow of color on the hardwood, but Van still felt chilled.

When she rounded the bed of her truck, she spotted the silver hairbrush and train case she'd meant to return to Natalie. Because of all the excitement last night, she had forgotten to bring it in. Since she had already locked the front door, she went around the side of the house and left the items on the kitchen table with a note, being careful to latch the back door on her way out.

Van didn't have too much time to worry. As soon as she'd set up the booth, the farmers market was swamped with locals and tourists. She was glad that she'd had the foresight to hire some help. It was difficult to think of darkness and hundred-year-old ghosts when the sun was bright and she heard nothing but happy chatter around her.

She took advantage of a small lull around ten thirty and called Natalie. When she didn't pick up, she felt some apprehension, but let it go when two more customers approached. Natalie was probably still sleeping.

❖

Natalie was headed to the kitchen to make coffee when the cold hit her like a sharp slap.

"Give it a rest, would you?" Natalie snapped. Her entire body hurt from her impromptu excavation of the fountain last night. She would have thought that doing another house cleansing would have, at the very least, bought her another evening free of ghosts.

She turned and saw the train case and hair brush on the table. The items that Van's crew found yesterday after an employee had been injured. Blood energy, she thought and felt the top of her head tingle.

The instant Natalie touched the silver handle, terror snapped at her senses and she experienced a flash of someone striking down at her face with the heavy brush. She stifled a scream and threw it across the room. She took some deep breaths and tried to shake off the residual energy attached to the object. How much pain had to be involved in an event that the echoes would still be felt over a hundred years later? Her heart ached for Beth and Sarah and she felt a surge of fresh hate for Richard.

Natalie gathered some wet paper towels and sat to clean the case. The old lock broke open easily after a hard twist. She sneezed, dislodging more dirt, and uncovered fancy initials etched into the inside of the lid. *S.S.* Sarah Seeley, Natalie guessed. She carefully reached inside, ready to pull away in an instant.

The basement door slammed and Natalie snapped her hand back. She heard a woman cry out as if struck. The cry became a plea and grew louder.

"Please, please help us!"

Natalie broke out in a cold sweat. For a moment, she wished frantically for her mother, and then admonished herself to be a big girl. She finally worked up the nerve to reach back into the case, finding only an old makeup compact and small bottles whose labels had disintegrated over time. When she carefully took them out and lined them on the table, she was disappointed to find the rest of the case empty. She thought for sure she was supposed to find something significant. Maybe it was a little foolish, but was it too much to hope there might have been a key?

After emptying out the dust and dirt, Natalie was curious when she felt a slight thud, so she shook it again. Yes, there was something definitely hidden in it. Using her sensitive fingers, Natalie felt around the bottom of the lining and found the tiny spring latch.

She flinched when the bottom dropped from the case and hit the floor. She set the case aside and gathered the bundle that had fallen out. Carefully, she unwrapped what appeared to have been black silk and discovered a small diary. Sarah's diary.

It was in remarkably good shape for being so old. Natalie was excited. She got her coffee, held the book close to her chest, and went into the living room to get comfortable.

Dear Lord, I was too late!

The Atlantic liner on which I was traveling was delayed by sea storms causing me to miss the train west. By the time I arrived, the wedding was over. I was barely introduced to the young bride before my brother pulled her away from the reception and other guests.

I was also completely unprepared for the absolute terror that Richard's mere presence still inspires in me. My blood still runs cold at the memories of his tortuous violations of my body and spirit.

I should have stayed in Paris. Yet, how could I live with myself if I didn't at least attempt to warn the girl foolish enough to marry the devil?

I was woken this morning by the sounds of Richard leaving the house with two large valises. I waited to see the young bride join him, but he left alone. I watched his back until he was out of sight, and it was at that moment that I heard crying.

I found poor Beth still lying on the floor of the master suite where he left her. There was so much blood! I wondered what on earth that little girl could have done on her wedding night to have my brother beat her so. The sight broke my heart, but it was the low keening that twisted in my heart and had me running to her side. I knew that sound well, and the resonance woke upon my soul the wounds still fresh under the scars that my brother bestowed upon me.

Beth's arms flailed at me when I held her and her heart beat fast and frantic in her chest like a baby bird's wings in great distress. I tried to soothe her and clean the blood as best I could while she still lay on the floor, unable to yet move.

Hours later, Beth stirred herself enough to help me get her into the washroom. It was then that she took off her tattered peignoir and I could see the full extent of her injuries. Black and purple stripes covered her thighs, stomach, and chest, her face swollen almost beyond recognition from the pretty young bride of yesterday. I could only stare in horror at vicious bite marks on her breast. She began trembling so I gently brought her to the bed that she never made it into last night. "Why?" Beth asked me.

Why indeed, because my brother is an evil, sadistic man. I could only wonder how this fragile young woman came to marry him in the first place. Through her battered lips she told me a story so horrible, I could only sit in silence until she finished.

Beth's father sold her to Richard! Actually sold her for his debts to the devil himself. Her mother passed away several years ago, and Beth grew up terrorized by her own father, much as I suffered Richard.

The horrible irony of it all is that she traded one monster for another. Her dream of escaping that prison and becoming the lady of the manor here has been brutally shattered.

I am greatly concerned at her lack of hysterics. She seems resigned to her lot. I cannot in good conscience leave her here alone with my brother.

I have to help her. We must plan an escape.

Natalie wiped at the tears drying on her cheeks. Those poor women! She couldn't imagine living in the age where a woman's value was decided for her. Her beautiful house had been the breeding ground for so much pain. Natalie's stomach hurt, but she wanted to continue reading and turned to the next entry, mindful of the brittle pages. There was a short notation that Richard had sent word to the women that he planned to stay in New York until his business was concluded and another on how well Beth's injuries were healing and she was beginning to open up.

With each page turned, Natalie could read between the lines written in Sarah's perfect script. Sarah and Beth became inseparable, turning the gardens into a masterpiece and sharing everything about their respective histories.

They took many long walks on the beach, which were described in great detail, but there was no mention of what they would do when Richard returned. Natalie felt helpless and wanted to scream at them to run away while they still could. She was sad for them and wanted to quit, but felt compelled to keep reading.

I'm in love with her. How can I state it more plainly than that? I pray that I can protect her until my plea reaches Aunt Tilly. If anyone can help us, it will be her. After all, it was she who saved me when I was eighteen. My brother would never cross her. She's far too powerful in her own right. I must stay strong for this gentle girl. I can only hope that Richard stays away until we make good on our escape.

Natalie yelped when the phone rang and barely kept herself from throwing the diary in the air. "Hello?"

Nothing. She was sick of this crap. She slammed the phone down on the coffee table and was surprised to see evening shadows across the floor. Just how long had she sat here anyway? She rubbed her stiff neck and stood to stretch.

The phone rang again and she gave it a dirty look, refusing to answer it. Natalie held her breath until the ringing stopped. The red message light began blinking. Did she really want to listen to it? What if it was Van? What if it wasn't? *Stop it!* She was driving herself crazy.

Loud, crashing noises came from upstairs and the windows rattled from the force of what sounded like a battle raging outside. Ice water flooded her veins and she froze in place while the noises continued.

My studio! The thought of anything happening to her paintings snapped Natalie out of her temporary paralysis. She raced to the top of the stairs and stopped outside the door. The second she put her hand on the knob, the noises stopped. Cold mist wrapped itself around her, the tendrils snaking through the hall behind her, almost snapping with small electrical pulses.

Natalie reached the top of the landing and looked around the room. *Oh, my God.*

The room was in absolute shambles, paint splattered on the walls, and art supplies were scattered across the floor. The armchair by the window lay on its side and her easel was broken into pieces and shoved in the corner. Natalie couldn't seem to get a grip on the reality of what she was seeing and she sank to her knees.

When her legs could hold her, Natalie wiped the tears from her cheeks and began straightening the chaos. The smell of turpentine filled the room while she cleaned the paint. She admitted to herself she was scared but continued to clean in a methodical manner, keeping her focus only on removing the mess and not the cause.

She was in the kitchen washing her hands when the phone rang. Natalie stared at it as if it were a snake ready to strike. This was ridiculous. She snatched up the receiver. "Hello?"

"Finally!"

"Mary, I'm glad to hear your voice."

"Is there something wrong with your phones?"

"I'm going to have to call the repairman to come out here and repair the lines." Natalie was grateful for the interruption. "How are you?"

"I'm good. Listen, one hour, chicken fried steak for dinner, it's your favorite, the boys want to see you, and I'm not taking no for an answer." Mary hung up.

Natalie chuckled. An evening with her extended family sounded like an awesome distraction. Maybe she could find some much needed balance and the dose of normality and stabilizing anchor she knew Mary could provide. She wondered if she should call Van and leave a message. Just what was the protocol here? Yes, they had gone to bed together, but that didn't mean they had to check in with each other. She hadn't called her all day so maybe she needed space, and realistically, could Natalie blame her after everything that was going on? Then again, her service had been so erratic, maybe she had? Natalie felt some of her old insecurities come knocking. Okay, she argued with herself, you are not going to sit at home by the phone and wait to hear from her. She did, however, make sure she had her cell phone before leaving.

❖

Van hit the emergency doors and raced to the front desk. God, she fucking *hated* hospitals. She and her crew were just packing up when she got the call from Uncle John telling her that Dad had been admitted with chest pains. She tried not to think about what she would do if she lost one more person she loved. She spotted her family grouped together in the waiting room.

"What happened?" she demanded when she reached them.

❖

The moon was so full when Natalie drove home, the light reflected off the dark water in the ocean, making it appear as if there were two yellow orbs. She had enjoyed herself at dinner and let Mary convince her that things weren't as scary as she thought. Some of this had to be a symptom of all the change in Natalie's life. It had been much easier to believe her logical explanations when she was sitting in Mary's bright kitchen than sitting in her own driveway. Natalie did her now automatic check of the front window.

All clear, she thought while approaching the front door. The front entry was quiet but not cold. Two more points to the positive side. Natalie checked the first floor, the second floor, and stopped at the staircase to her studio. The door was shut. Leave it alone, she decided then headed for her room.

No scent of lavender, no doors or windows opening. The air felt clear and light, but she lit the white candles on her nightstand anyway. Natalie let some tension slide from her shoulders. She got ready for bed then checked her messages. No word from Van. She tried not to feel apprehensive. How awful would it be that she finally found some passion and affection only to lose it? That would be worse than never having it at all. She knew what *that* felt like, and how could you miss something you never had?

Natalie lay awake listening for noises in the house.

She must have dozed off because the candles were out. Natalie turned over and saw a fire burning in the hearth, casting shadows on the walls. She attempted to sit but felt heavy and lethargic.

"I'm talking to you. Wake up bitch."

Natalie opened her eyes, once again lying next to Beth and trapped in her memories. Richard looked down at them with a predatory smile and she felt bile rise in her throat. "Please, just let me know if there is any word from Sarah and then leave me alone."

"I told you that she wouldn't look back. She did the same thing when she turned eighteen." Richard's eyes narrowed and Natalie felt the cruel fingers that roughly pulled Beth to a sitting position as well as the bruises on her body from her last beating.

"She wouldn't leave without saying good-bye."

"Did you think she actually cared about you? You, a worthless, stupid bitch? Or did you think she would take you away with her?"

Beth didn't answer, just hung her head. Natalie could feel the tears that spilled over with the hopelessness that overwhelmed her.

"I would kill you if you left. I would hunt you down and fucking murder you, do you hear? I own you, remember?" Richard pulled back his arm to make a fist.

Beth screamed and curled to protect her stomach. "The baby! Don't hurt the baby."

"Don't hurt the baby," Richard mocked in a high voice. "It better be a son and not a stupid cunt like you are. I might just kill you both." Richard shrugged into his coat and grabbed his hat. "I can't even stand to be in the same room with you. You're pathetic." Dark shadows swarmed around his retreating figure.

Natalie held her breath and waited for the door to close. Beth cried next to her and rocked back and forth. "She said she loved me. Why did she leave?" Fresh grief stabbed Natalie's heart.

"Sarah? The baby just kicked."

Natalie realized she could feel the strangest sensation. She put a hand to her stomach. It felt like the flutter of a butterfly against the inside of her skin. Beth began humming while she rocked. "Hush, little baby, don't say a word."

Natalie felt her heart crack when she recognized the lullaby.

CHAPTER FOURTEEN

Van was exhausted from sitting up all night with her father while they waited for the test results to come back and a specialist to arrive. They were relieved to find out it was nothing serious, but the doctors decided they were going to keep her father for observation for several more hours. She couldn't go home until she checked on Natalie, whom she knew must be sleeping. She would just take a quick peek. After finding her crying in the studio and then again outside in the rain the previous night, she felt she had to make sure she was safe.

Van stood in the dark kitchen to let her eyes adjust, but when she started for the stairs, she felt the air get thick and cold. Her steps were heavy and in slow motion. She tried not to panic as she attempted to run. This was the stuff nightmares were made of. Nausea rose and stole her breath; her legs wouldn't go any faster than a slow crawl, and her muscles burned with the effort. Sweat trickled down her neck, and icy fingers tap danced on her spine. The staircase grew taller right before her, and for every tread she managed to climb, it seemed ten more were added to the top. She tried to yell for Natalie, but the only sound that would come out of her throat was a harsh whisper. The illusion of the never-ending staircase shattered into pieces and Van fell onto the landing, gasping for breath. She gained her feet and raced for the bedroom.

Van stood in the doorway and tried to reconcile her brain with what her eyes were seeing. It wasn't Natalie's room, the one she spent the night in. She looked over at the unfamiliar bed. There was a small shape huddled under the blankets that shook with small, wounded sobs. "Natalie?" She ran to the bed and tried to throw the covers off, but she was horrified to find that her hand went through them. The bedroom door slammed and Van spun around, fists clenched, legs steady, ready to fight. A man approached her and flipped his hat onto the chair, shedding his long black coat as he came closer. He was a big man, but not much taller than her. She held her defensive stance. She noticed his dark eyes and a scar that ran down his sharp cheekbone toward the corner of his cruel thin mouth. Rough stubble colored his face. He moved past her and sat on the other end of the bed.

He yanked the covers and exposed the woman who appeared to be hiding.

Van blinked. It wasn't Natalie. The woman's long dark hair was tangled in the sheets and she was curled up to protect against the attack. Van couldn't see her face but could only assume that this was Sarah and her brother Richard. The dark man. *Shit.*

When Richard fisted his hand in Sarah's hair, Van's head snapped back and her eyes watered from the pain. "Leave her alone!" she yelled and swung at him, nearly falling when she spun with the force.

"Wake up!"

Van blinked and looked at Natalie's concerned face above her. Her heart was racing and she felt completely disoriented.

"You scared me to death."

"What happened?"

"I went to bed alone and woke up with you screaming next to me."

Van sat up and realized she was under the covers. Had she simply crawled into bed next to a sleeping Natalie and been dreaming? Her hands were shaking, but she rubbed her temples and tried to comprehend what just happened.

Natalie got on her knees and curled up against Van's back, her body heat warming the chilled skin. "When did you get here?"

"I was just coming to make sure you were okay. I didn't mean to intrude, and I don't remember getting in the bed." Van wondered just how many lines she crossed by letting herself in. She simply hadn't thought about it while she was focused on Natalie's safety.

"It was certainly an interesting way to wake up, and you're not intruding. I appreciate your concern, but where were you that you came in so late?"

Van checked the clock. Damn. It was already ten in the morning. She told Natalie about the night with her father in the hospital.

"Why didn't you call me? I would have come. Is he okay now?"

"They said I could take him home this afternoon. He'll be fine. He may not like slowing down or changing his habits, but he'll be okay." She didn't tell Natalie how scared she'd been sitting there next to her pale father. It reminded her too much of Cara's death, making grief feel fresh and new all over again. By the time they got the test results and knew her dad was okay, it was too late to call.

Then the dream put sharp hooks back in her. "Get dressed," she ordered Natalie. "We're leaving and going to my house."

"Why?"

"Just get dressed." Van told her what occurred on the stairs and what she had witnessed in the room.

"But that doesn't make sense. Why would *you* start seeing Richard and Sarah?"

"Natalie, none of this makes any sense. Trust me when I say, I don't know why, I didn't ask for it, and I want to leave."

"I'm not running away," Natalie said.

"You need to come with me. It's. Not. Safe. Here," she said slowly, as if she were talking to a child.

Van noted Natalie's stubborn chin and knew she didn't have time to argue. She didn't even want to, for that matter. She had the same look herself. She shook her head and sighed. "I have to go back to the hospital and bring my dad home. Do you remember how to get to my house?"

"Yes."

"If you change your mind, the extra key is under the blue pot to the left of the mailbox on the front porch." Van hugged her. "I'd feel a lot better if you were safe at my place until we figured this crazy shit out."

❖

Van helped her father up the stairs.

"I'm not an invalid. I can walk," he snapped.

"Quit being so cranky, old man. You scared the crap out of me, so let me take care of you, dammit."

"I'm not cranky; you're smothering me, Miss Attitude."

Van considered her mood and decided she was justified. First for the panic she'd had over her father, next for having spent the night in that poor excuse for a chair, then there was the nightmare at Natalie's this morning.

She bullied her father into taking a nap, and after making sure she was covered downstairs in the nursery for a few hours, she decided she should also try to rest. Just how weird was this going to get? Not only had she experienced the footsteps and rattling doors, now she had experienced the dreams. Sarah's past. What was *that* about? Was it because Natalie was already connected somehow with Beth, and now Van got the leftovers? The questions were enough to drive her crazy and piss her off.

Van thought if she were smart, she would run the other way. Fast. Really, really fast. Her logic and emotions warred with each other. As much as she wanted no part of the ugliness she witnessed in her own dream and those that Natalie told her about, Van wanted to believe that Natalie needed help, needed *her*. It had been so long since she'd wanted to be needed by someone that it felt almost alien. She could only hope she was strong enough to help her.

Van pulled the blankets back on her old twin bed and fell asleep the second her head hit the pillow.

Natalie took her coffee cup and Sarah's diary outside with her. She curled up on the glider and turned to her bookmarked page. She refused to give up hope that she might find some clues on how she could help. She had to find some resolution for the ghosts in the here and now knowing that she'd either go crazy trying or have to sell her beautiful house.

> I came to this morning with a splitting headache and my face is swollen and purple. Richard was in a temper last night and went after dear Beth with his fists. When I tried to stop him, he only beat me down too.
>
> How could I forget how cruel he has been to me my entire life? It's as if his fists have jarred my memories. Things that were better left buried in my mind. When I was thirteen, he locked me in the root cellar beneath the basement after our parents left for a tour of Europe. How could I have not remembered that? I can only speculate that it's because of the trauma involved.
>
> I screamed until I was hoarse, pounding on the cement walls until my fists were bloody and I finally passed out from exhaustion. Three days he kept me locked down there. Three days without food or sunlight. He took great pleasure in tormenting and humiliating me while he used my body for his own deviant needs.
>
> He finally let me out in the middle of the night and brought me to my room. He'd left my beautiful kitten dead in the middle of my bed and warned me that I would be next if I told anyone. He must have threatened the servants as well because none of them ever said a word about my disappearance.
>
> He has locked me in my room and I believe he's going to kill me. If I can't get out and get help, he's going to kill Beth.
>
> I think he knows that we have become lovers. Perhaps I was too careless with my touch around the servants and they have told him.
>
> I hear him on the stairs.

It was the last entry in the diary. Natalie flipped through the pages. She felt unspeakably sad and let her tears fall unchecked while she curled in a ball and rested her head on the arm of the glider and closed her eyes.

Natalie slowly became aware of the rhythmic thunder of waves rolling on the beach. Now what? She rubbed her eyes when a figure emerged from the fog and she squinted to focus. Beth approached her and motioned her to sit in the sand. Natalie wasn't frightened, just curious. "This has got to stop."

Beth looked directly at her. "I want to help you, Natalie."

"Then stop these nightmares, please." Natalie reached over to touch her and wanted to panic when she felt warm, solid flesh. "Am I dead? Where are we?"

"Between," Beth said and waved her hand impatiently. "But that's not important."

"Excuse me; I think it's pretty damn important. You've been dead a while. I have a life."

"Richard is more powerful now. He has gathered the strength to manifest."

Natalie thought of her trashed studio. "Apparently. How do I get rid of the bastard?"

A smile spread on Beth's face. "I wish I could have had your spunk back then. We might have run away or managed to kill him, one of the two."

Natalie stared at Beth. It was more than a little eerie, like looking into a mirror image that had a life of its own, separate from reality.

"I've waited so long for you to come back."

"Yeah, about that. Why me? What about the others that used to live here? How come they never saw you or Sarah?"

"They weren't you," Beth said simply and shrugged. "You are the key."

Natalie was exasperated. "The key again. *What* fricking key?"

"It's the blood."

"Excuse me?" Natalie's stomach filled with dread, just as a chill covered her damp skin. "What was that again?"

"Can't you see it?" Beth's form began to shimmer and fade.

"Don't you dare leave me hanging. Clarify this for me, please?"

Beth's voice was a whisper in the breeze. "You are the blood of my blood. *You* are the key."

"But that also means..." Natalie didn't even want to say it out loud.

"Richard is your great-great-grandfather."

Natalie realized that she was staring at the waves crashing on the beach. She felt dazed and her mind raced fifty miles an hour and on five different tracks. She didn't remember leaving the house; let alone descending the steep stairs to the sand. Good Lord, she could have drowned herself. She had to be at her breaking point.

She turned to look up at her house, and even though she felt the sun warm her shoulders, she shivered. She brushed the sand off her ass, wincing when she felt the granules in her scratches.

Natalie turned back to look at the waves, perfect in their synchronicity. Her life used to be that ordered. In appearance, anyway. She inhaled the sharp, salty breeze and followed her own footsteps back the way she'd come.

Natalie skirted the rear of the house and let herself in the front door then crossed the hall over to the bathroom, pulling wet, sandy bandages off as she went. The scratches looked good. They were healing fast. She looked into the mirror and the full impact of what she experienced struck her between the eyes. *Richard is my great-great-grandfather? What kind of shit is that?* She shook her head to clear the blurred image. For a second there she thought she was staring at Beth. *Are you sure you're not just going crazy, Nat?*

Then realization hit her. She was related to Sarah as well as Richard and Beth. Things that make noise in the night, okay, she could go with that. Weird dreams, okay, she could run with that also. Apparently, she could also take poltergeist activity in stride. But this? The whole dead ancestor thing was freaking her out. Is this why she could feel them so strongly? Was it really the blood that coursed through her veins?

How much of her life was her own? How did she happen to purchase the very house that her great-great-grandmother owned with her sadistic husband? Natalie was stubbornly refusing to acknowledge the fact that she and Richard were related. That was too terrible to think about right now. It would have to be on her father's side, as she could trace her maternal ancestors clear back to County Clare, Ireland.

The visions were longer and more intense, the story gathering momentum with each dream. There was so much going on right now that she was having a hard time remembering who she was before the divorce. Did it matter? She was here now.

Blood is the key, Beth had said. Well, Natalie thought, I've invested some. She knew instinctively that this haunting was going to take a lot more than burning sage and lighting candles. She didn't know the details yet. She planned on calling her mother, if she could get through, and asking her to dive into Dad's family tree. The more information she had, the quicker she could get to the bottom of things, and the sooner she could get on with her new life.

Natalie wasn't going to let anyone, let alone a ghost, dictate any part of it. Life was for the living, and her dead relatives weren't going anywhere. She packed up her fear and made a decision to go to Van's.

Natalie found the key where Van said it would be, unlocked the door, and went exploring. She admired the stainless steel and modern design in the kitchen and wandered back out to the living room. The walls were a light camel color that set off the black suede sofa with the chaise on the end. Two dark red leather armchairs rounded off the other end. There were bursts of red and orange in the pillows and accessories. The fireplace was gorgeous and looked to be the restored original rather than a replacement. Natalie breathed deeply. The house smelled like Van, and it made her insides flutter. She lifted her brow in amusement when she saw the game equipment hooked to the television hanging above the fireplace.

The house suited Van perfectly. Beautifully masculine, yet underscored with soft touches here and there. She ended her tour in Van's bedroom, pausing at the dresser to look at the framed photographs. There was a young girl dressed in a softball uniform holding up a trophy for the photographer to memorialize. She looked at a virtual life collage of Van in all her sports pictures, showing how lean and athletic she had always been. Natalie was tickled to note that even as a teenager, Van had bigger muscles than her ex-husband. There was another photo of Van and her father sitting on a pier with fishing poles strung out over the water. It all looked so Norman Rockwell, she continued to smile.

Ah, here it is. She picked up the photograph of Van laughing with another woman. The love in her face radiated outward. Cara had long, dark curls and brown eyes that appeared to be filled with mischief. They had their arms around each other and they looked impossibly young and happy. Natalie felt a flash of sadness for the girls in the picture. What would that have felt like? She believed for years that she loved her husband, but she knew they'd never taken a picture like this together. Natalie gently replaced the frame and went to lie on the bed. She was unbelievably tired, and it was no wonder, as she hadn't had any decent sleep in days.

Tonight, she would concentrate on Van. After that, or better yet, tomorrow, she would get busy on a list of things to be done and write out in detail what she could remember of her dreams. It would all wait. It had been waiting for years.

She rolled over and tried to push all the dark, racing thoughts out of her mind and just relax. Easier said than done, but in spite of the inner turmoil, she felt herself starting to float easily before she fell asleep.

❖

Van pulled her truck in the driveway and laid her head back for a second. Between the scare she'd had with her father and

Natalie and her crazy house, she was exhausted. In addition to that, she had meetings with three suppliers today, each of whom tried, unsuccessfully, to raise their prices. She looked at her filthy clothes. Maybe she could grab a shower before dinner. She noticed Natalie's car on the street. In spite of how tired she was, Van wondered if she could charm Natalie into said shower with her.

Natalie opened the door before she got to the porch. Van stopped to look at her and her breath caught. Her hair was loose around her face and she was wearing a white tank top and cropped yoga pants. Unexpectedly, her throat closed with emotion. She hadn't had anyone she wanted to come home to for a long time, and she didn't realize until that very moment how much she had missed it.

Natalie smiled slowly with a small question in her eyes. "Hi," she said, "I made myself at home like you said. Actually, I've slept most of the day."

Van smiled. "Hey, honey, I'm home."

Natalie opened the door wider and went out on the porch to hug Van. "How's your father?"

"Cranky as hell, but well. I'm dirty," Van said, pulling away from her slightly.

"Okay," said Natalie and hugged her anyway, burying her nose in her neck. "You smell good."

"I smell like work."

"You smell like sunshine baking on naked skin. I love that."

Van made a purring sound in the back of her throat and pulled her close. "Oh yeah?" She kissed Natalie's soft neck. "You smell like…mine."

"What an incredible thing to say. Do you have any idea what you do to me?"

"I hope it's at least half of what you do to me." Van looked down at Natalie's open face, her beautiful eyes heavy with brimming tears. "I hope those are happy tears," she said, running a finger gently under Natalie's lower eyelashes.

"What I'm feeling is so big, I don't know where to put it all."

"Aw, that's easy, honey." Van led her into the house. "Let me show you."

❖

Van started the shower, stood in the bathroom, and stripped. Natalie felt herself flush and immediately felt the heat between her thighs. Her skin tingled in anticipation as she watched Van step under the spray.

Natalie stared at the blurred flesh-colored image through the frosted glass and swallowed. Van peeked out after a second. "Feel like getting wet?" She crooked her finger at Natalie.

Natalie hesitated for a moment then laughed. "I believe, ma'am, that I already am."

Van grinned wickedly. "Show me. Come here." She stood aside to give her room to get in.

Natalie quickly took off her clothes then pressed herself against Van's wet back. When she moaned at the contact, Natalie felt the sound travel straight to her center and she shivered. There it was again, that wonderful surge of sexual power. She reached around Van to get the soap and a scrubby hanging on the wall. Natalie's breath quickened and her nipples went taut.

The sight of Van standing spread-eagle with her perfectly sculpted arms high on the shower wall, hands flat against the tile was incredibly erotic. She was so beautiful, Natalie could only stop and appreciate her. Van turned to look over her shoulder. "What?"

"You're perfect."

Natalie heard Van's quick intake of breath. "Don't move." She lathered the soap, and beginning at Van's neck, she slid the foam along her skin in long strokes, finally dropping the scrubby because she didn't want anything between them.

Natalie continued to stroke Van until she heard her strangled gasp when she reached around to caress her breasts, rolling her nipples between her fingers. Natalie moved her own naked and wet body against hers, marveling at how amazing the friction felt.

Van tried to grab her, but she was too slippery. "Uh, huh," Natalie said. "My turn." She wasn't going to let Van distract her. Until this moment, it was always Natalie on her back and on the receiving end.

Natalie got down on one knee, and then the other, keeping her eyes on Van's. "Let me taste you." Natalie moaned when she felt Van's hot flesh pulsate against her lips. She'd hoped she would be good at this, and seeing and feeling Van's reaction told her she was.

Natalie pressed more hot kisses then let her tongue explore and taste. God, she was so soft. Her hands grabbed Van's ass to bring her even closer. When she found the rhythm that had Van moaning the loudest and squirming against her tongue and teeth, she doubled her attention and increased the tempo. She dropped one of her hands to the ache screaming between her own legs and stroked herself. Van's thighs trembled then tightened and Natalie felt her orgasm down to her own core and she came with her, nearly blacking out in the process. Van turned off the water and slid down the wet tiles to sit next to her. Natalie folded her up in her arms and loved feeling the pulse in her neck beat erratically because she knew that she made it happen. It was an amazing feeling. She couldn't wait to do it again. "Chinese food," she said.

Van laughed. "We deliver."

Natalie covered her face in kisses.

Later that night, Van lay awake in the dark with Natalie curled next to her, head on her shoulder. She could smell her shampoo and the love they shared. She smiled at the ceiling recalling their lovemaking. Wherever she turned, Natalie was there, wherever she wanted to go, Natalie went with it and then took her there as well. She was proving to be a little sex goddess. As if Natalie could read her thoughts, she sighed and held her tighter. Van's heart swelled. She had thought she would never know this feeling again. Her thoughts stopped cold, and her body went from relaxed to coiled and tense. She knew this feeling. Van had been in love exactly one time before. Lust, plenty of times, but this, this feeling she knew well. She had worked hard over the years to never even get close to it. Love meant pain, excruciating pain. And loss. And yet, hadn't the good years been worth it? For the first time in a long while, she could remember the joy that being in love brought.

She searched her heart and yes, incredibly, she had fallen for Natalie. If she was honest with herself, and she usually was, she had known Natalie was different that first night on the beach. Love at first sight she reasoned, and Van was lucky enough to have experienced it twice in her lifetime. She turned Natalie onto her side and curled to spoon behind her. Tomorrow held promises she hadn't dared to hope for in years.

Chapter Fifteen

Natalie was surprised when she woke up refreshed. No dreams or flashbacks during the night to haunt her. She carefully unwound herself from Van's embrace and pulled a T-shirt over her head while she padded into the kitchen to make coffee.

When she pulled a stool up to the counter, she spotted Van's bullet list she'd made the other night when they laid out the events that had occurred in her house. Natalie had refused to talk about any of it last night. She put her energy instead to pleasing Van. She felt herself blush when she recalled how many ways she'd found and loved.

Natalie sighed happily. The coffee smelled wonderful.

"Hey." Van stood in the doorway wearing boxers and a thin ribbed tank. Natalie felt her nerve endings wake up and tingle pleasantly.

"I'm sorry. Did I wake you?"

"No, the bed got cold without you. What are you doing up so early?"

"I'm adding another revelation to our connections. I didn't tell you about my last experience or even touch on what Sarah wrote in the diary I found in that case."

"Another one? What happened?" Van kissed the top of Natalie's head then filled two coffee cups and brought them over. "A diary?"

"I'll be right back." Natalie ran back to the bedroom to get Sarah's book out of her purse. When she returned, she paraphrased the contents for Van then flipped to the last entry. "Richard kept Sarah prisoner in the root cellar. Do you think—"

"Here's how I see it," Van interrupted. "I've taken the day off. We can beat our heads against the wall trying to solve your mystery, or we can forget this for a while, be normal, and spend the day together doing whatever feels good—without any dead relatives from the past and without poltergeist behavior going on over our heads. What do you think?"

Without waiting for Natalie to answer, Van tossed the book onto the counter then slipped her arm under Natalie's legs and headed to the back of the house.

Natalie laughed and tried to pull her shirt back over her naked thighs. "Stop it; I'm not wearing any panties."

Van chuckled. "Even better."

❖

Van came out of the bathroom and felt a wave of tenderness at the sight of Natalie lying sprawled across the top of the bed mumbling into the sheets. "What's that, sweetheart? I didn't hear you." She leaned closer and Natalie sprang, catching her by surprise, and pinned her to the bed.

"Water," Natalie said. "Need water." She fell back on her side.

Van went to the kitchen to get her some and when she returned she found Natalie fast asleep. She drew the sheet over her and decided to make them something to eat.

At the doorway she turned for one more look. Natalie took her breath away. Stole it, just like that. Van teetered on the razor edge of panic. What if she lost her? Logic told her it was an old fear, but her heart still cried in the shadows of her grief over those she had loved in the past and lost.

She pulled the bacon from the refrigerator and glanced at the clock. Well, not breakfast time, so she'd make a late brunch. While the bacon was frying she thumbed through Sarah's diary. Van couldn't imagine living in those times. She couldn't understand it at all.

Something kept nagging at her conscious, but every time she tried to focus on the thought and figure out what it was trying to tell her, it slipped away again.

"Smells good in here."

Van hadn't heard her get up. Natalie crossed the room to her looking very young with her hair pulled into a high ponytail and wearing Van's T-shirt again. Natalie's nipples showed through the thin material and Van reached for her.

Natalie laughed and danced away. "Uh, huh, you have to feed me before ravishing the body again."

Van smiled. "Ravishing?"

"Don't you read romance novels? Never mind. How come all women aren't lesbians?"

Van nearly choked on her coffee and raised an eyebrow.

"I mean, I know I've asked before, but is making love *always* like this? I feel kinda ripped off for all the years I've wasted. I think at one point this morning, I forgot how to breathe."

Van thought of the empty sex she'd been accustomed to. "I think that when it's just physical, it doesn't touch your soul. It's like our spirits recognized each other, and making love is our soul's way of rejoicing." Van shut her mouth. Where the hell had that come from? She'd never spoken so esoterically in her life.

Natalie put her fork on her plate. "That is, without a doubt, the most wonderful thing that anyone has ever said to me."

The phone rang, making them both jump.

"Don't answer it." Natalie stared at the ringing phone like it was a coiled rattlesnake.

"It might be my dad." Van reached for the receiver. "Hello?"

Nothing.

"Hello?" Van strained to hear who was on the other end. She wasn't sure, but it sounded like someone was screaming in the background far, far away. Her heart began to accelerate. "Freak."

A male voice broke through the static, low and guttural. "Bitch."

"What did you just say?" She was ready to disconnect when the voice on the other end bellowed so loud she had to hold the receiver from her ear.

"Stop fucking my wife."

"Who is this?" Van felt as if someone had just thrown ice water in her face.

Silence.

"Hello?" The phone went dead. "Asshole," Van said and clicked the off button. She looked up and saw the look of absolute horror on Natalie's face. "Nat? It's okay, honey. I'm right here."

"Did he say what I thought he said? Did he say 'stop effing' my *wife?* Did I hear that right? Tell me he didn't say that."

Van didn't answer. She had absolutely no idea what she could say to make it better. This situation was so beyond her scope of reality, she couldn't wrap her mind around it. She was so high on this new relationship she hadn't really dissected what had happened in Natalie's house, let alone the fact that the dark man was calling her, and at her home instead of Natalie's. She tried to be reasonable. "Nat? Do you think that could have been Jason?"

"Who?" A quizzical look crossed her face. "My ex-husband? Oh yeah, him. No, that wouldn't have been Jason. There is nothing confrontational about him whatsoever. Besides, how would he have gotten your phone number? He's married to someone else now, remember? This is so…so…I don't have any words to explain it other than unbelievably unreal. I don't know how much more of this that I can handle, Van. I really, really don't."

Natalie disappeared into the hallway. Van followed her to the bedroom and heard the water turn on in the shower. She looked helplessly around the room and at the door closed between them. *Screw that.* She opened the bathroom door and looked in. Natalie was curled in a ball on the tiles in the shower, sobbing quietly, her shoulders shaking and her arms wrapped tight around her stomach. The sight of it broke Van's heart and she climbed in to hold her, clothes and all.

Chapter Sixteen

"I have to go home, Van," Natalie said. "I have work too."

"Can't you paint here?"

Natalie saw the concern in Van's expression, and who could blame her after the way she'd fallen apart yesterday. She was still a little embarrassed. Natalie didn't want to think of herself as emotionally needy, though she had appreciated the comfort.

"Van," she said gently. "I'll be fine. The crew is going to be there, right?"

"But—"

Natalie kissed her. "Have a good day. Say hello to your father for me." She left quickly before Van could continue the argument that started half an hour ago.

She waved to Rick and smiled at the continued progress they were making. After a quick house inspection and finding nothing out of place, Natalie felt her shoulders relax a little. She went into her office to e-mail her mother since Richard appeared to be blocking their phone communication. Natalie gave her a quick rundown of the activity and told her of the bombshell Beth had dropped on her. The screen flickered.

Oh no, you don't, Natalie thought and hit send. She felt a burst of triumph over the small victory and brought her optimism with her to the second floor throwing her bedroom windows open to the spring air.

And because that felt so good, she did the same thing in the guest rooms.

No more darkness, she thought, automatically repeating the chant that usually accompanied the sage ritual. Only light and love were welcome here.

"This is *my* house, Richard. I will love who *I* choose." She paused and held her breath, almost waiting for a reaction. When there was none, her mood continued to rise.

She changed and went to her studio. Damn, she'd forgotten her easel was broken. She ignored the hair rising on her neck and crossed to the closet, pulling the long chain that turned on the bare light bulb. She stepped in to get her old easel when she tripped over something and landed painfully on her knees. Natalie sat and swore while she rubbed them then noticed the loose floorboard.

It was probably stupid to look under it, she told herself. *Curiosity killed the cat*. The old wives' tale popped into her head and she remembered the next line. *But satisfaction brought it back.* This was Beth's old studio when she was alive; maybe *she* had a diary hidden in here.

Natalie pried the first board out then recalled Van's father and his story about Richard locking himself up here. She felt cold chills run along her back and hesitated.

She'd never know if she didn't look. Natalie lifted the second board cautiously, leaning away from the hole in the floor, just in case. She laughed nervously. In case of what? In case Richard jumps out? The possibility sounded ridiculous, even to her.

A glint of gold in the corner caught her eye and she reached in to pull it out. It was an old locket. She ran her finger over the delicate roses etched into the front of it. After a quick study, she found the tiny latch, opened it, and gasped when she found the human hair. Red and dark brown locks braided together in a strand small enough to fit inside the locket. Her fingers tingled and grew warm. It had to be Beth and Sarah's hair. She carefully tucked it back inside.

It was such a tragic love story, yet in spite of their circumstances, they had loved each other deeply. The locket was a symbol of that.

Natalie returned the board and got her easel out. She still had that third painting to finish. She decided that the third would be the sketch she'd done of them on the chaise. It didn't fit into her series, and it was different from her trademark solo women. But her life was different now and she wanted to give Sarah and Beth to each other, in today's world, where they might have been able to love each other in peace.

Tears threatened to blur her vision, but Natalie wiped her eyes and started to paint.

❖

It was late afternoon before Van was able to break away from her father and the nursery. When she got to Natalie's, the front door was unlocked and she went in. "Natalie?" She received no answer at all on the first floor. After searching the second floor, her anxiety increased until she reached the door to the turret studio. A small note card was taped to the outside. *Do not disturb.*

How cute was that? Van thought before quietly climbing the stairs. Natalie stood at her easel, paint smeared on her face, and her eyes looked almost wild with her intense focus. Her hair was escaping the ponytail she wore and curled around her neck. Van could hear the whisper of the paintbrush as it flew from the tray to the canvas then back again. She noticed the open windows and the afternoon breeze had turned the room chilly. "Natalie?"

"*What*?" Natalie shot her gaze to Van. The hard, impatient look in her eyes made Van take a step back.

"I didn't mean to interrupt you. I was worried when I didn't hear from you today."

"Working here." Natalie tilted her head to the side and stared back at the canvas.

"I can see that." Van smiled. "Can I look?"

"No."

Really? Van thought, just like that? The finality of that one word stopped her in her tracks. Natalie continued to paint as if she weren't in the room. Yet another slice to add to Natalie's personality.

"Van? Don't take this personally, but I need for you to leave now. I'll call you later."

Now, that one stung. Van had certainly never expected this scene on the way over. Well, Van knew a brush-off when she heard one. Don't call me, I'll call you. She'd said the same words to others plenty of times. "Fine. I'm leaving."

By the time she hit the front door she was seething. Van had only run over here to check on her and her fucked up house. This feeling of rejection wasn't setting very well for her. As a matter of fact, Van was the one who *did* the backing off. Here's your hat, what's your hurry?

The anxiety she'd carried all day had completely transposed to anger on the drive home. See what happened when you stepped outside the boundaries and got too close to someone?

She was in her driveway when Annette called.

"Hey, stranger, where you been?"

Naked Natalie smiled in her mind. "Around."

"Come out and play, Easton. The girls are wondering if someone snatched your fine ass up."

Van snorted. Snatched and tossed, she thought. "Miss Apples?"

"Yep. We'll be waiting." Annette hung up.

A beer and a friend sounded good right now. Just the things to get her mind off of Natalie and the emotional roller coaster Van had been on in the last few weeks. She knew there were plenty of women who would love her company. Caring about someone took too much energy.

❖

Natalie's eyes burned and her arm ached when she finally dropped her brush into the jar of turpentine. It was nearly two in the morning. A dull throb in her temples and the gnawing in her belly sent a reminder she hadn't eaten since the previous night.

She resisted the urge to inspect her work. She'd learned over the years that if she didn't walk away from a painting at some point, she would never finish it. Instead, she went to her room and dropped into her bed fully dressed.

❖

"I'll take her home," Candy offered.

Van closed one eye and tried to focus. It didn't do much good; there were still two of her. "S'okay," she slurred. "I'm good."

Annette smiled at her and took her keys. "I got her," she said and helped Van to her feet. "It's been a long time since I had to pour you into bed, my friend."

Van gave her a sloppy kiss. "My buddy."

"Say good night. We're out of here." Annette steered her to the door of the tavern and nearly tumbled when Van spun around to wave at the stragglers behind her.

"I can fasten the seat belt by myself." Van batted her hands away and rolled down the window to let the cool breeze in. "God, I'm drunk."

"I knew that when you started line dancing."

"Now you're lying to me. I don't dance."

"Actually," Annette said, "you were kind of cute out there shaking your booty."

Van groaned. "Shoot me." She winced because now she could recall a spin that had her crashing into a table. She was pretty sure there would be bruises the next day. She asked herself if it was worth it. Her head was spinning and the whole purpose of going out and getting blitzed hadn't worked. "Want to see Natalie. Take me up there."

"I don't think she'd appreciate your charm right now, pal." Annette patted her shoulder. "Sleep it off and call her tomorrow."

"Love her," Van said. "But she threw me out." Annette helped her into the bathroom and into bed. Van kept one foot on the floor.

"Hurts." Van rubbed her chest.

"Your head is going to hurt like hell in the morning," Annette said. "Do you remember the sculptress I used to date?"

Van grunted.

"Well, when she was working—creating as she called it. There could be an earthquake and it wouldn't shakc her focus. She threw a cutting tool at me one time."

"Want me to kick her ass?" Van started to rise.

Annette laughed. "Old history, Van. My point is that artists can be temperamental and moody to us mere peasants."

"Natalie told me that once." Van tried to open her eyes. "Here, in my bed."

Annette pulled the sheet over her. "See? As long as she doesn't start throwing sharp objects, you're good. I'm leaving now. Good night, buddy."

"G'night." Van passed out.

Natalie was freezing. She'd forgotten to close the windows before she went to bed. Was it really noon? She tried to rub her eyes and found her hair stuck to her face in the paint she'd splattered. Her head was foggy when she stumbled into the shower and she stood under the massaging stream of water to loosen her sore muscles.

She closed her eyes, and in her mind's eye she could see the painting she created. Beth and Sarah on the chaise, full lips an inch apart, sharing that intimate breath the second before the kiss that would come. Their eyes were half lidded but full of passion that seemed to fly off the canvas. Beth's hand cupped Sarah's breast while Sarah's lay on the curve of Beth's hip. Their legs intertwined under white silk. Natalie had even painted the small gold locket nestled in the hollow of Beth's throat. Now that she had immortalized their love, could they find peace?

Natalie stepped out of the shower and pointedly ignored the mirror. She didn't want any messages this morning. She wrapped herself in a towel before heading to her dresser. The scent of lavender filled her room. She paused at the open window to look out.

Van was in the yard leaning on her shovel, her eyes covered in dark glasses. Natalie looked behind her to see what she'd just finished. Purple lavender and blue lobelia lined her walkway up to the porch.

"Good morning!" Natalie shouted out the window.

Van looked up, as did several of the guys on the crew, and Natalie realized she was hanging out of the window in her towel. She pulled it tighter and motioned Van to come inside.

She was in the kitchen when Natalie came in. "The flowers are beautiful, thank you." She crossed the room to start the coffee and chattered happily. "I painted most of the night. I think it's my best work." She turned to see Van still standing stiffly at the counter. She hadn't moved. Natalie hugged her, but Van's arms stayed at her sides. Natalie took a step back. "What's wrong?"

"You tell me."

Natalie was puzzled. "What happened? Is it your father? Is he okay?"

"Dad's fine."

"Then what?" Natalie couldn't read her with her sunglasses on. "Could you please take those off?"

Van set them on the counter. Natalie took in her bloodshot eyes and dark circles. "Wow, what did you do last night?"

"Went out with my friends."

"Okay." Where was this cold shoulder coming from? "So why are you mad at me?" Then she remembered Van coming into the studio and her response to the interruption. "Please tell me you didn't take that personally."

Van's expression told her that was exactly what she did. "Oh, honey, I'm sorry. I'm not used to anyone coming in when I'm painting. Jason knew better."

"I'm not your ex-husband," Van snapped.

"No, of course you're not, and I was rude. I apologize." Natalie was contrite. "It was not my intention to hurt your feelings."

Van had already reached that conclusion this morning when she woke up with a mariachi band playing in her head. Right now she was a little annoyed that Natalie was so chipper and Van felt like climbing into one of the holes she'd dug to die in peace. This time she returned Natalie's hug.

"Are you hungry?" Natalie asked.

The thought of food activated her gag reflex. "I could use some toast."

"I can manage that."

"Dry please."

"That bad?" Natalie smiled and looked sympathetic. "Are we okay?"

Van thought of how miserable she'd been the night before. That was the thing about feelings—when you turned them back on, you felt all of them, good or bad. They came back intensified to an almost unbearable degree. The alcohol hadn't helped that one little bit. "I—we're fine," she mumbled. She had almost said I love you but stopped herself.

She didn't object when Natalie brought her aspirin and ordered her to take a nap. Van thought briefly about setting a bad example for the crew, but she was hung over enough not to care. The guys would probably high-five her, thinking she was getting lucky. She'd deal with it later. She pulled the pillow that smelled of Natalie under her head and closed her eyes.

Her mouth filled with the unmistakable copper taste of blood. Van tried to roll over but found she couldn't move. God, she was going to choke on it. She opened her eyes and Richard stared down at her.

"I told you to quit fucking my wife."

She felt pressure around her throat. Her pulse roared in her ears while she tried to pry his hands off her neck. Suddenly, his weight shifted and she turned to spit while still gasping for breath. A punch to her kidneys sent white bursts of pain to her head. Van tried to roll away, but a kick to her stomach stopped her in motion.

Where was her strength? She felt weak and battered. She tried to talk, but no sounds came from between her swollen lips.

"I don't know what else I could expect from you, a whore's bastard. You're no better than our slut of a mother, spreading her legs for the fucking gardener."

Richard pounded her head against the floor. "I'm certain you didn't know that did you?"

Van felt her cheekbone crack under the next blow, tasting fresh blood when her nose broke.

"Oh yes," he said an inch from her face. "Father knew and forgave her, claiming another man's bastard child as his own. But I heard them fighting about it, oh yes, I did. The servants talking about it behind their hands." Richard opened the door and continued to drag Van out of the room. She looked frantically for something she could use as a weapon, anything.

His laughter bounced off the walls, growing louder in volume until she thought she would crack from the din. He was truly insane.

"Blood tells, Sarah." He pulled her roughly to her feet. "You should have stayed away. Now I'm going to fix Father's weakness and Mother's sin. You should have never been born."

Van struggled to get loose. She couldn't believe what she was hearing, couldn't focus through the pain. Richard shook her until her teeth rattled then she felt herself fly through the air when he pushed her down the stairs.

❖

Natalie checked her computer then opened the e-mail from her mother.

> Natalie, what's wrong with your phones? Been trying to reach you. Is everything okay? Got your message and I'm researching through your father's family tree. Remember all the papers he inherited when Aunt Edna died? Looking for clues. Will write when I find something. In the meantime, be careful. Anytime a blood connection is involved, the more powerful the energy. Love you, Mom.
>
> P.S. Your dad is ornery but doing well. He sends his love and is happy that you're happy.

She hoped her mother would find something that would finally free her house from Richard's grip. Natalie answered more e-mails and updated her webpage. When she heard the trucks leaving, she was surprised to see how much time had gone by. She hadn't heard a peep from upstairs. Van must have been exhausted with that mother of all hangovers. Of course, their late nights could have something to do with it as well, she thought.

Natalie opened the front door to admire her flowers. She was excited to find the lantana bushes in pretty pots on her porch. The blooms had always reminded her of the colors of ice cream sherbet. She sat on the top tread of the stairs to breathe in the afternoon air and appreciate the trimmed back oleander trees. She had just decided to go in and make dinner for Van when she turned and walked straight into her. Natalie let out a half-scream. "God, you scared me." She looked at Van's expression. If anything, she looked worse than she did before she lay down. "Van?"

"I want you to go and pack a bag and come home with me tonight. Right now."

Natalie felt the hair rise on the back of her neck and arms. "What happened?"

"Trust me, please. I'll tell you on the way." Van went back into the house.

Natalie's first reaction was to dig in her heels, but she did trust Van and did what she'd asked. She tried to reason with her fear but only felt it grow with each second that passed. She threw in some toiletries and hurried back.

Van met her at the stairs and they both jumped when a crash came from the kitchen. Natalie started toward the sound, but Van pulled her to the door. "I have to see." When she saw the stony look on Van's face, she relented and followed her to the truck. What happened to Van during the afternoon while she was online?

The ride home was silent. Van couldn't wrap her mind around the dream and its implications. On top of that, she'd never been so afraid or felt so helpless in her life. She'd always been strong and assertive, sure of her place in the world. Even when they had received

Cara's test results of the malignant tumor and her impending death sentence, Van hadn't felt so powerless. Yes, it was a physical enemy they couldn't fight, but this—this feeling of being at the mercy of someone else, someone much stronger—she had never felt before. She felt violated and the experience crossed boundaries in her that she hadn't known she possessed. Whether it was real or not, the remnants of Sarah's terror left her nauseated and shaky.

Van heard Natalie follow her into the bathroom where she wanted to wash off Richard's filth and Sarah's blood from her mind and body. "Give me a few minutes, okay?" she asked Natalie before stepping into the hot stream. She let the water and silent tears cleanse her.

The water ran to cold before she felt well enough to get out. Natalie wasn't in the room. She found her in the kitchen making omelets.

"Better?"

Van sat at the set table. "Sorry."

"Can you talk about it now?"

Though she'd rather not, Van described her dream. She felt almost disconnected from it now, reciting it as if it happened to another person, which, of course, it had. Van ate automatically, hardly tasting the food. But with each bite she took, she felt a little better, a little stronger, and a whole lot angrier.

Natalie cleared the table then returned to sit in her lap, curling against her. "Does this mean we're related somehow?"

"If we're to believe some insane man that kicked my ass in a fucked up dream, it makes us some kind of diluted cousins, I think," Van said.

"Sounds like the plot of an old and very bad movie of the week."

"Except we're living it."

"Or reliving it, as the case may be." Natalie laughed weakly then stood. "This doesn't change how you feel about me, does it?"

Van held her hand and pulled her back to her side. "Apparently, I loved you then." She met Natalie's gaze then held it. "And I love you now." She watched Natalie's eyes fill then gently kissed her, hoping that Natalie could feel through her lips what she felt in her heart for her. Natalie swayed slightly and Van steadied her. "And no asshole bully is going to tell me different."

Her breath was soft against Van's cheek when Natalie whispered, "Thank you." Then she led Van back to the bedroom.

Natalie lifted her arms while Van slowly lifted her shirt over them. "What's this?" she asked, tapping the small locket.

"A piece of who we once were," she answered then took it off and set it on the dresser. "But tonight, it's who we are now that matters." Natalie felt a little dizzy. Van had said she loved her. Though she knew she loved her too, she wasn't entirely sure she trusted it yet. Words were easy. Hadn't Jason told her that he loved her just the day before she learned Tracy was pregnant and he left her?

Instead, Natalie swallowed her own words and trailed her tongue between Van's breasts while running her hands over the curve of her ass. She loved everything about her. When Van picked her up, Natalie expected to be thrown down to the bed and covered with Van's weight. But she laid her down gently, holding herself a few inches above her.

Every movement was slow and unhurried. Van's lips and hands caressed Natalie's skin until she was in tears and completely undone. Still, Van moved sinuously against her, in a sensuous dance of slippery bodies wet with passion. Her tongue was everywhere. Natalie felt as if she were floating in an otherworldly place where only sensation and Van existed.

Chapter Seventeen

Natalie stood at the back door and sipped her coffee. Right now, right this very minute, she didn't remember ever feeling so complete. The sun was brighter, the birds sang in harmony, and the warm spring air smelled like heaven. It was a morning full of promises.

The sound of a car door slamming brought her to the living room where she saw a tall, blond woman coming toward the front door. It was that bitch from the boutique, and Natalie flushed with anger. What the hell was she doing here? She opened the door and startled the woman who had yet to knock.

"Can I help you?" Natalie asked icily.

The blonde quickly composed herself and narrowed her eyes at Natalie. "Wow, she's quick. Gotta give her that."

Natalie felt her heart start to drop like the New Year's ball in Times Square. "Excuse me?" She was shocked to see the house key the woman was holding in her manicured fingers.

"Candy," she snarled. "The name is Candy, and I had no idea I was going to be replaced so quickly." She tilted her head to the side and studied Natalie. "And by a redhead, too. Now, that—that just stings." She showed no sign of recognition that they had met before.

"Replaced?" Natalie tried to find her bearings. Anger, shock, betrayal, all recent friends, came back to slap her. She ran her hands nervously over Van's shirt that she'd put on earlier.

Candy smirked at her. "Yeah, I liked that shirt too. Although, I do have to say, generously, in fact, that color looks better on you than on me." She let out an evil chuckle. "Of course, we were a little drunk the other night; I didn't wear it for long."

The morning lost its joy and Natalie felt hollow. "What do you want?"

"Well, I wanted a piece of ass, but it looks like you got here before me. Not into sloppy seconds, not even for Van, so I guess I'll wait."

Natalie sputtered and felt as if she'd been dropped into the middle of a play and didn't know any of her lines. "Wait? Wait for what?"

Candy tossed her hair over her shoulder and laughed. "Oh, you think I've lost Van to you?" She backed down the walkway. "I haven't lost my girl, honey; I've just lost my turn." She sashayed back to her car, leaving Natalie standing in the doorway, her heart in pieces at her feet.

❖

I haven't lost my girl; I've just lost my turn. The words pinged around and around Natalie's heart, caught in a loop that came back to hit her, again and again. The jarring bells on her cell phone interrupted her dark thoughts. She checked the number, hoping for her mother or Mary. It was Anton from the gallery. Twenty minutes later, she got off the phone with a promise to deliver the two paintings she did have completed. Without telling him what was actually going on, she explained that she just wouldn't be able to finish the third one as promised. He accepted the deal that she proposed—four paintings for the next show in the spring, and no, he didn't care that she didn't know what the subjects were yet.

Natalie tried dialing her parents' house again. There was still no answer. On another impulse, she attempted to call Mary's cell phone and it dropped into voice mail. She didn't leave a message. She'd known that the other shoe would drop; she just hadn't thought it would drop so soon. What was it with her? Did she have a big sign on her forehead that said cheat on me? And why did this hurt more than her ex-husband's betrayal? Shouldn't twelve years stack much higher than a few weeks? Apparently not.

She was unbelievably hurt but packed her few things quickly, shutting the door behind her. She hadn't left a note, and why on earth should she? She thought of all the lies and excuses that Jason had given her over the years. She would not give Van a chance to do the same thing. She was done with lying, cheating, sons of bitches, male or female.

❖

Van paused before the automatic doors, dreading the thought of going into yet another hospital. Oh, this one was disguised as an assisted-living facility, but the sounds and smells were exactly the same. She checked in with the front desk before continuing to her grandfather's rooms. After discussing what she had learned with her father earlier that morning, he had suggested she come and talk with him.

The dream grew claws and it wouldn't leave Van alone. When Natalie had told her about the dreams she'd had, on one hand, Van could sympathize with her fear. But on the other hand, when she'd experienced one for herself, that powerlessness shook the foundations of who she believed herself to be. It took things to a whole new level for her.

To be honest, she was pissed off. If spirits could invade her dreams and shift fate, how come Cara had never come to her? When she died, Van's heart shattered into tiny pieces of glass that pierced her soul until the pain was so great she would have welcomed death as well. If ghosts could communicate, how could Cara have *not* comforted her?

Van tried to put it aside. She would probably never know. She survived it.

Her grandfather was in his favorite recliner, wearing a light blue cardigan that Van knew her mother had made years ago. She searched his face, trying to gauge where his mind was, and if he would recognize her this time.

"Vannie!"

"Hey, Grandpa." Even if she knew the Alzheimer's was responsible for his memory, it still hurt when he didn't know her. The disease didn't affect the family member who loved the person, and she hated it for stealing her grandfather's faculties and wonderful memories they shared. She was so relieved that he seemed to be present today.

Van settled into her visit. It was only after they talked of sports, the weather, and how well the nursery was doing that she steered the conversation to the past. "Did Dad tell you that I'm doing the gardens at the old Seeley place?"

His face lit up. "My grandfather used to work there."

Van smiled. "I know. What was he like? I don't know much about him."

Her grandfather clasped his hands and closed his eyes. "He was a handsome man, of course. He was an Easton." He laughed. "He didn't have much of a formal education, but he was the smartest man I ever met. He could make anything grow, Vannie, anything at all. He never had a harsh word for anyone. Everyone loved him."

"Did he ever talk to you about the years he worked there?"

"Well now, let me see if I can remember."

He sat so still Van worried if his mind wandered and she'd lost him. But after a few moments he began to talk quietly.

"There is a little cove hidden in the rocks nearby the Seeley house where Grandpa used to take me fishing. Every time we passed the area, he would point and talk of the fairy gardens. Oh, how he loved this story.

"'Once upon a time,' he always started it that way. There was a princess that lived in the tower, trapped into a marriage with a much older man that her father made her marry. She would weep in the tower because she was lonely and missed her family."

Van leaned closer, entranced by the story and his soft voice. She almost felt the waves rocking under the small fishing boat and could see him as a small boy fishing while listening to his beloved grandfather.

"One day, she came upon the king of the fairies, making the flowers grow in his garden. The sight of him frightened her so badly, she ran away. But she couldn't stop thinking of the handsome king of fairies and sought him out.

"They fell in love, as princesses often do with fairy kings, and she wasn't lonely again."

He stopped talking and Van tapped his knee. "Then what happened, Grandpa?"

He smiled. "Well, I suppose they lived happily ever after because that's the end of the story."

No, they didn't, Van thought. Her heart hurt for the great-great-grandfather she'd never known who told his little grandson about a great love disguised as a fairy tale. She wouldn't mar his memory in any way and ask if he knew that his grandfather had loved a married woman and possibly had a child with her. It wasn't anything that anyone could prove.

"I have to leave now, Bella." Her grandfather stood. "Chores to do before Pops comes home. Thanks for your help."

Van felt a painful tug. Bella, her grandmother. Her grandparents had known each other since they were nine years old. He had that look in his eyes. The one that said he'd gone away to a place he called sometime yesterday.

His smile was so guileless, so bright, that Van couldn't help but smile back even as she felt the weight of sadness settle on her chest. "Bye, Gramps. I love you."

He looked confused for a second before he sat in his chair then looked out the window, rocking back and forth, humming a tune she didn't recognize.

Van let herself out.

❖

The tow truck pulled into her long driveway and Natalie stared at the front of her house. She wondered if it was her imagination or her heartbreak that created the dark cloud that appeared to be hanging over her roof. She could do this. In fact, she thought, I've already done it. Hadn't she been in the exact same place only a little while ago? She opened the truck door and quickly thanked the driver, handing him a twenty dollar tip. Cold and icy rain drops bit her face and hands, soaking her before she could reach the door.

She shook off in the foyer and made a mental list. The first thing she needed to do was to call the gallery and tell them she couldn't make it. The mechanic told her it would be at least a week before they could get to her car. She had no idea what was wrong with it. She had been on her way back home from Van's to pick up the art she was going to deliver and the car just quit running. She pulled to the side of the road and tried starting it again. Nothing. It didn't click like it would when her battery went dead. Fortunately, she was only two blocks from Bayside Auto Repair. The tow truck driver brought her home and said he would tow her car on the way back to the garage.

She was grateful for the sudden rain shower. It would delay or, *please, God*, cancel Van's work crew. She didn't want to deal with any of it. Van had told her how superstitious the workers were, and right now, she knew any excuse at all would keep them away. That was fine with her.

"It's just me," she called out. *Who are you talking to?* The house was quiet. Her footsteps echoed on the hardwood while she checked the house. She cautiously peeked around the doorways. Nope, no nasty surprises. Natalie finished her route, let out a sigh of relief, and her shoulders came down off her neck.

She felt hollow inside and knew herself well enough to get busy and try to get her mind off the blonde who ripped the rug out from under her. *Candy. Bitch.* Or should she place the blame right where it lay? With Van? By her own admission, she slept around. Natalie didn't understand that behavior. How could she sleep with Candy one night and tell her she loved her the next night? She knew that she wasn't experienced the way Van was about sex. But how could she hurt her that way? Their lovemaking meant something to Natalie; it meant everything. She just assumed because of her own strong feelings that Van felt the same way. Assumed, there you go, made an ass of herself, again. Natalie refused to cry and pushed the tears back. She was so tired of hurting.

Natalie flipped on the stereo to cover any unexplainable noises on her way to the phone and dialed the gallery. Their machine picked up so she left a message, quickly apologizing for the delay, and explained what happened to her car that morning. She promised she would call the art moving company to deliver the paintings at her own expense.

A phone call to the company brought a promise to pick up her paintings the next day. They assured her they would make certain the pieces were delivered as soon as possible, relieving her of some of the guilt pounding at her temples. It did nothing, however, to relieve the icy fingers that tapped on her spine or the hurt constricting her chest.

The rain continued to pelt the windows and the wind rang the new chimes she'd hung on the porch. She didn't want to give in to despair, but she felt a little lost. Her grief hadn't healed completely from the first betrayal before Van left fresh tracks over the top of it.

What if *all* of this was a dream?

Her door was shut, and after entering, she checked the window. It was still latched. In fact, nothing seemed to be disturbed at all. It was still a little messy when she packed in a hurry the night before, but other than that, there were no surprises. Natalie climbed into the unmade bed, she didn't want to think about anything or anyone; she just wanted to get some rest. She curled into a tight ball and while she rocked herself to sleep, she finally let the tears come.

It was dark when the sound of soft sighs and moans woke Natalie. The room gradually lightened until through the shade of purple twilight she could make out two figures on the bed. The stab of betrayal in her stomach constricted as she watched the women make love. How could fate be so cruel, to give her something so wonderful, to have it ripped away? The sound of the front door slamming made her jump. She looked over to Sarah and Beth, but they appeared not to have heard it. "Get up!" she shouted, and shook the bed. "He's coming, hurry." The room grew cold and Natalie shivered. "Beth, Sarah, hide! He's almost here."

Natalie's heart pounded harder with each approaching step from the hallway. "Please, please. He's coming." She begged the women in the bed. Nothing worked. She knew with a horrified certainty what was going to happen next, and she was powerless to stop it. Sarah was leaning over Beth, softly talking to her while she stroked her.

At the same moment that Beth threw her head back against the pillows, her face filled with ecstasy, the bedroom door slammed open. Natalie threw herself back against the wall. She inwardly cringed at the look of contorted rage on his face. "I caught you!" Richard reached the bed in three quick strides and pulled Sarah off the bed by her hair. She swung helplessly in his grip and tried to reach for Beth. "You're fucking my wife? You sick bitch, you are going to pay for this. You bring this unnatural act to my house?" He shook her with each word he spit out at her, until her legs went out from under her.

Beth cried and pleaded with him to let Sarah go. "Please, Richard. I'll do anything. Just let her go." She crawled on her belly toward him. "Please."

"You disgust me, whore." Richard stood with rage radiating from his eyes. The only sound in the room was his heavy breathing and the sobs from the two terrified women.

"You'll do anything? You will pay for this until the day your miserable, pathetic life ends." He threw Sarah down on the floor and ripped the sheet away from her when she tried to cover herself. He turned toward Beth and ordered her into the bathroom.

Beth slowly stood. She kept her eyes down and her head lowered in submission. "What are you going to do?"

He didn't answer, but roughly grabbed her by her arm and forced her into the bathroom. His fingers dug deep into her naked arms. After he threw her in, he shut and locked the door. "Do not move!" he yelled through the door. He stomped back to where Sarah was crumbled on the floor and hissed at her. "Pack your bags. You're leaving. I don't ever want to see you again."

Sarah looked up at him hesitantly and gradually got to her feet. She reached for the nightgown hanging on one of the bottom posts of the bed and quickly pulled it over her head. Sarah started to back out of the room step-by-step, as if unwilling to turn her back on her brother. She made it to the door then Natalie could hear the sound of her bare feet running in the hall.

Richard watched her go, and an evil roar ripped from his throat, chilling Natalie to the bone, almost choking her with fear. Natalie huddled on the floor and cried with her hands over her ears in an attempt to muffle the pitiful screams that reached her through the closed door of the bathroom.

❖

Van sat with her father on the wide porch, watching the rain and rocking companionably while they talked about her visit with her grandfather.

"It makes me sad, Vanessa, that we may have had a relative that we know nothing about."

"We can't prove it, Dad."

"That doesn't make her any less ours."

"No, you're right. It doesn't. Boggles the mind, doesn't it?"

"That it does, baby." Her father continued to rock in his chair in a slow, steady motion.

Van drew comfort from his nearness, grateful that she had always known how much she was loved. Home was a safe place full of love and laughter. Her father's recent health scare only made her more determined to completely break out of the protective shell she'd built around herself. "I love you." She patted his knee. "I'm going to take care of some paperwork."

"Love you back. I'm just going to sit here awhile longer."

Van kissed his cheek and went into her office to pay the monthly bills. The business line rang and she picked it up automatically. "V & V Landscapers, how can I help you?"

"Van? This is Mary, Natalie's friend?"

"Well, hello there." Van put the pen aside and leaned back in her chair.

"Have you seen Natalie? I've been trying to call her all weekend and all I get is a bunch of static. Wherc is she and what have you done with my best friend?"

"Whoa. Hang on. I can see why you and Natalie are best friends. Do you guys always talk that fast?"

"Don't have time for small talk. Answer me."

Van relayed to her what had been happening with the phones.

"So where is she?"

Van held her annoyance because she could hear the worry in Mary's voice. "I left her sleeping in my bed this morning."

"You're sure she's all right?"

Van smiled. "She's fine."

"What exactly are your intentions?"

Van couldn't help it; she laughed out loud. "Oh, are we going to have *that* talk? Is this where you threaten me with bodily harm if I hurt her in any way?"

"God, I'm sorry. Did I sound that crass?"

"Yes, but being that you're her best friend and you're worried about her, I'll forgive you."

"Can I have your home number so I can try getting a hold of her there?"

Van rattled off her number. "But I've been trying all morning, and she isn't answering there either."

"I'll try again. If she's still not picking up, I'll swing by her place and see if she's there and let you know, okay?"

Van said that was fine and disconnected. As long as Natalie stayed at her house and didn't go home alone, she wouldn't worry. She looked forward to sharing what she learned today with her this evening and then they could get busy with the whole kissing cousins situation, she thought, amusing herself with the analogy. She looked back at the stack of bills and sighed before getting back to work.

The door to the bathroom opened and Richard threw Beth on the bed. His face was set in hard lines and his shirt splattered with bright

red stains. He didn't even look back before he left the bedroom. Natalie pulled herself off the floor, using the bed as an anchor. She peered at Beth and her hand flew to her mouth in horror. Beth lay unconscious, her blood soaking into the sheets that had so recently given her pleasure. Natalie could only stare at her helplessly for a moment until she felt her fear drain away. Red hot anger came in its place, until she felt it pulsating in her veins. Rage tasted like copper in her mouth.

Natalie turned from the bed and followed Richard's path out the door. He was at the end of the hallway, heading for Sarah's room. He didn't appear to be in any hurry, just stepping heavy as if he were drawing out the terror that Sarah would be feeling as he approached. Natalie ran toward him so fast, she felt like she was flying.

Richard spun and grinned. His face began morphing between himself and the demon that he was. She was momentarily surprised he could actually see her, but Natalie didn't even slow her approach. She came at him, screaming with fury. A split second before impact, Richard sidestepped to the right. Natalie ran straight into the wall and hit it full force, turning the world black.

❖

Van was out in the greenhouse helping a customer when she saw Mary waving a hand above her head and heading toward her. She quickly excused herself and met her halfway. She was a little startled when Mary hugged her, but she returned the hug. Mary followed Van through the store. Van had to stop now and then to let her exclaim over the various lush plants and art pieces on the shelves.

"How come I didn't know this beautiful yard stuff was here?" Mary stopped to look at a blown cobalt glass ball being held aloft by an exquisite fairy.

"Maybe because, I don't know, I might be going out on a limb here. You've never been here?" Van laughed and continued to the office.

Mary stopped in front of a display that held several large wind chimes, and poked a finger to make them ring. "I want one of these!"

"We'll grab one on the way out. Let's talk back here."

"Very nice," Mary said as she looked around the room that held flowers and artfully arranged crystals and knick-knacks.

"Thank you. Please sit down."

"I probably could have called, but I wanted to check the place out. The gallery Natalie works for called me trying to find her to let her know that her room reservations had been confirmed. Evidently, her phone is still out of order and they were looking forward to seeing her this evening."

"Oh," said Van. Natalie had never said a word to her about leaving. She didn't know what to say.

"Maybe she tried, you know, phones out, and all. She probably left you a note or something." Mary stopped and looked over her shoulder. "Do you hear that?"

Van's nerves twitched. "What?"

"I thought I heard someone crying." Mary put a finger to her lips to gesture for silence and listened for a few seconds. "I must have imagined it."

After she walked with Mary to her car, Van found the wind chime that she had admired. She took it to the front counter, handed it to the clerk, and told her wrap it up so she could surprise Mary with it later.

Why hadn't Natalie tried to get a hold of her to let her know she was leaving? The nursery was on the way out of town. She could have stopped by. Van felt a slap of insecurity. Natalie hadn't told her she loved her back last night. Should she assume that the declaration had scared her off? Natalie didn't owe her any explanations, yet Van still felt hurt that she wouldn't say anything to her about where she was going. Should she give Natalie her space? Following a sixty second argument with herself, she dialed her number anyway.

Still no answer.

CHAPTER EIGHTEEN

Natalie opened her eyes, shocked to find herself sitting on the basement stairs. Her thin shirt stuck to her perspiring skin, sending icy chills over her body. The last thing she remembered was running into the wall and blacking out. Her pounding heart signaled her fear; she could hear the pulse of it in her eardrums, shutting out all other sound. Why was she down here? She gradually became aware of another noise, and heard a faint voice muttering. She forced herself to look around. The clean concrete floor was missing as well as the bright fluorescent lighting. It was dark and gloomy; cobwebs scattered on the rafters like crazy spun sugar. Natalie realized she was going to have to play this nightmare through to its conclusion. She was aware of the cold but knew it had nothing to do with the chills she was experiencing. Every hair on her body stood up to signal danger. She moved in and through the shadows, trying to reach the source of the racket. Fear curled in her belly and prickled on her skin. When she got to the last stone pillar, she cautiously peeked around it.

Richard was busy raking the dirt floor in the west corner, giggling and talking to himself. Natalie was certain he was insane. She crouched by the pillar to watch and see if she could make out what he was saying. She froze when he turned around and looked directly at her. Natalie didn't even blink; she let fear hold her immobile.

Richard shook his head and poured fresh dirt from an old bucket over the mound he'd already smoothed, stopping to check his work every few minutes and wipe the sweat that broke out on his forehead. "Fucking bitch tried to stab me. Who the hell does she think she is?"

Natalie noted the blood drying on his cheek. What had he done with Sarah? Then she realized he must be covering the entrance to the old root cellar. She had wondered when she did the first walk-through why her old house didn't have one but figured the previous owners had filled it in. She gagged when she realized he might have buried Sarah in there. The horror of the situation hit her, but it was still anger that drove her to action. Natalie looked for a weapon she could use. If he could hurt her, she should be able to hurt him too, right?

She turned and saw a two-by-four leaning against the pillar. She quietly picked it up and pulled it behind her head. She advanced to Richard's back while her pulse increased double-time. She felt she would only get one good shot. When she was directly behind him, she swung with all her strength, only to find herself on the floor, having spun a three-sixty, right through his visage.

She ran that around in her mind for a second, even while her hip hurt from the landing, she hadn't even touched him. The only conclusion she could come to was it must be that she couldn't change the past. These events had already happened, and no matter what she did or what she attempted to do, it could have no bearing on history.

From her position on the floor, Natalie could see blood running down the side of his neck soaking into the collar of his white shirt to mix with the sweat from his exertion.

Natalie's heart broke for Sarah, but she couldn't help or save her, not even while she was seemingly trapped here in this loop of the past.

Van kept busy after the rain stopped trying to keep her uneasy feelings at bay. But no matter what she did, she couldn't seem to shake the sensation that she was being watched.

She finished stocking some new inventory and then spent some time pacing her office, willing Natalie to call. Hell with it, she thought. There was no sense in forcing herself to stay until the nursery closed.

In fifteen minutes, she was on the road home. Natalie's car wasn't in the driveway and the anticipation and hope she carefully built over her nervous stomach plummeted.

There was no note. Van searched the house twice, feeling the emptiness of the rooms increase with each pass through them. Natalie's unique scent lingered in the air, almost mocking her. She couldn't think of a single reason why Natalie would have left without saying good-bye. She sat at the kitchen table and her gaze wandered over to the trash can in the corner. Inside it was a swatch of blue that made her curious enough to investigate. She found one of her shirts hanging half in and half out of the garbage. Van was certain it was the shirt Natalie had been wearing that morning.

Richard finished raking the dirt and stepped through Natalie. Still curled on the floor, she watched him go to the stairs and waited for the door to slam. It felt like she'd been stuck in this dream forever. It certainly seemed like she was awake. The cement floor was cold under her body and her palm stung where a wood splinter pierced her flesh. She wondered how long she had been out. Finally, she couldn't take it anymore; she crawled over to the fresh dirt she knew Sarah was imprisoned under. She hesitantly stretched out a hand and touched the mound. Her heart skipped when her hand passed right through it. Did she dare?

She had a weird flash of Alice falling through the rabbit hole, but she had to find out. Natalie took a deep breath and fell…into the small cellar where by the light of a stubby candle she saw a bedraggled figure huddled against the dirt wall. Natalie crossed to her on her hands and knees. Please no, she thought. Please. Dark, matted hair covered her face, but Natalie knew who it was. She pulled Sarah's head into her lap to look at her, only momentarily surprised she could make physical contact. She was aware of wetness seeping into her jeans, and her stomach heaved when she realized it was Sarah's blood. Natalie's heart cracked and she felt grief start to bloom in the fissure. Small at first, it grew with each tear that fell; until she was sobbing and rocking Sarah's body as if to comfort them both. Natalie wasn't sure if it was her grief or Beth's or maybe a combination of both. The sound of her keening filled the small dirt space with sorrow.

Natalie gently pulled Sarah's hair away from her battered face, placing a soft kiss on her forehead to say good-bye. It wasn't until she turned her lifeless body over that she saw the broken tines of a silver fork sticking out of Sarah's chest. Oh, baby, he killed you with your own weapon? Natalie was fiercely glad that Sarah stabbed him first. Hate bubbled in her veins and continued to heat her blood until it reached the top of her head, where she felt it become almost palpable in the small space.

She crawled a few feet away from Sarah and stood, taking note of the blood she wore. Natalie was enraged, threw her head back, and screamed. "Richard! I'm coming for you, you son of a bitch!"

❖

Van's head was resting on her folded arms when the phone on the counter rang causing her to jump. "Sweet Jesus!"

She rapped her shin against the barstool, fumbling the receiver. "Ouch! What?" She snapped into the phone then realized it could be Natalie and softened her tone. "Natalie?" There was a pause on the line then what sounded like a sigh of resignation.

Van held the receiver tighter to her ear while she tried to rub her bruised shin. "Honey?"

"You used to call me that."

Crap. "Candy." The night they were all out at Miss Apples, Van had tried to ignore her blatant advances. She was pretty sure she had made herself clear that she wasn't interested, so why was she calling? "What's going on?"

"Is the redhead still there? Or is it safe to come over now?"

"What are you talking about? What do you mean is the redhead *still* here?"

"The one you apparently dumped me for."

"What? I didn't *dump* you, Candy. We weren't in a relationship, and you know it." Van knew her well enough to know it was simply her pride that was hurt. She had probably soothed that injured ego with at least three others since Van.

"True." Candy laughed. "But I *miss* you, baby. Get rid of the old lady and I'll come back."

Puzzle pieces came together for Van. *Back.* No note saying she was going anywhere, no answer to any of her calls, shirt in the garbage. "Did you come over earlier?" *Oh, poor Natalie.* She could just imagine how Candy acted; the girl was so full of herself. Panic started simmering in her belly. "Candy, what did you say to her?"

"Oh, come on, does it matter? Whatever. What time should I be there? Got some bubbly and a new red negligee."

"Goddamn it, Candy." Van pinched the bridge of her nose and tried to rein in her temper. Had she really spent time with someone so shallow?

"Well, you don't have to be rude about it. You know what? Keep her, Van. Yours isn't the only phone number I have. It isn't even at the top of my list. Just don't expect me to come running the next time you're crying in your beer."

Candy hung up on her. Van waited for the dial tone and dialed Natalie's house then cell phone to listen to the now familiar never-ending ringing. "Damn it!" She only needed to talk to her, to explain. She hadn't done anything wrong, but she felt guilty anyway.

Van grabbed her keys and raced for the driveway. She had to find her.

❖

Natalie's primal scream pulled her into a spinning vortex where sight and sounds sped by in an instant.

"Stop hitting my mommy!"

Natalie was still dizzy, but she clearly heard the little tearful voice. Henry? Turning toward the sound, she saw a small boy running. He threw himself on Richard's back and began to beat his tiny fists on his head. Richard stood from his crouch with the little boy still attached.

Beth lay on her back on the floor. She reached out a shaky hand, pleading with Richard. "Please don't hurt him. He's just a little boy."

He roared for the nanny. She came running out of the nursery with her little white hat askew. When she reached them, Richard plucked Henry off his back and thrust him at her.

"Mommy's been bad, and I have to punish her."

Henry reached out his little arms to his mother. "Come with me, Mama."

"Go with Nanny, Henry. Mama will be in later to tuck you in."

Natalie watched the boy being led quickly down the hallway, but he kept looking over his shoulder, never taking his eyes off his mother.

Beth painfully tried to get her knees underneath her. She hung her head and Natalie watched bright red spots drop onto the hardwood floor. Richard yanked her to her feet by her hair. "You will not turn my son against me." He shook her.

"You do that all on your own, Richard." Beth's eyes were dry and her face calm while she spoke freely. "It is you and your actions that breed the hate in this house."

Natalie watched her stand straight and tall. "You will die alone and unloved, haunted by your evil deeds." Beth's expression seemed to shoot fire at Richard, and in an act of complete never-seen-before defiance, she spit her blood into his face.

Richard tilted his head to the side, staring at her blankly until his mouth split into an evil grin. He laughed, big, rolling bellows, and slapped the sides of his legs. Suddenly, he stopped, the smile disappeared, and his cold eyes looked calculating. "Sarah asked for you." He pulled something out of his coat pocket.

Beth's face radiated with desperate hope. "Sarah?"

"Right before…" He leaned in and grabbed her by the back of the neck and hissed in her ear, "I killed her." He threw a lock of long brown hair at her.

"What did you just say?" Beth shook her head and crossed her arms over her stomach.

Richard started steering her toward the bedroom. "Conversation is over."

"No!" Screams bubbled out of Beth's throat. One after the other, the shrieks of denial rang through the hallways and echoed back. "You bastard!"

Richard backhanded her in an effort to silence her, but it had no effect. Beth tore into him with her nails and teeth. He grunted in surprise but quickly overpowered her and threw her back onto the floor, then stood over her prone body.

Beth lay on her back for a few moments before slowly and painfully getting back on her feet. She threw her head back and screamed one last time then went eerily silent. Her cheek was rapidly swelling and Natalie could see the blood that pooled in the corners of her mouth. Beth looked utterly calm. She looked in the direction her son had gone and pressed her fingers to lips, blowing a gentle kiss.

"Sarah never left me." Beth pressed herself against the wall, took a deep breath, picked up the hem of her dress, and in three strides, threw herself over the balcony in a swan dive, still clutching the lock of Sarah's hair.

Richard loped down the stairs, whistling under his breath. Natalie rushed to the railing, horrified to see Beth crumpled and broken in the foyer, blood already pooling beneath her body. When she saw Richard unceremoniously grab Beth under her arms and drag her to the front door, her knees buckled and she fell to the floor.

❖

Van drove for an hour and a half along the coast before she came to her senses and stopped on the side of the Interstate. What would she do when she reached the gallery Natalie was headed to? It was simple enough to find the address, but it would be the middle of the night by the time she got there. Was she going to sit outside until it opened? She had no idea where Natalie would be staying and couldn't reach Mary to ask.

Van pounded her steering wheel, frustrated that she'd have to turn around and wait. Patience was not one of her virtues, especially when she felt she needed to fix something. Her stomach twisted when she thought of how hurt Natalie must have felt when Candy showed up at the house.

She wondered if it was karma for the way she'd casually used and discarded women in the past. Yes, she was honest and told them upfront she wasn't interested in a relationship, but deep down, she knew that she'd hurt a few along the way. Van had justified and rationalized her behavior for years, using her grief as a weapon and excuse for her actions. She hadn't considered anyone else's feelings but her own.

Van turned her truck around at the next rest stop and headed home with guilt and shame riding shotgun beside her.

Natalie raised her head and realized that she had been sleeping at the kitchen table. She looked around—her own table, in her own time, thank God. Her back was stiff and her neck hurt. A fire burned in the hearth, but she knew she hadn't started one.

"Look at you. You're pathetic. You're an *unnatural* bitch just like those two whores."

Natalie whipped her body toward the sound of his voice. She instantly felt her temper snap, her hate dismissing the fear that threatened to close her throat. "Well, *Gramps*, you're a sadistic, murdering *asshole.*"

Richard's red eyes bored into her and he let out a short bark of laughter. "They deserved it. Didn't or wouldn't know their place at a man's feet."

Natalie was exhausted and just wanted all of this to be over. "What is it that you want? Why don't you just stay dead and rot in hell where you belong?" He snapped his fingers and the fire went out, leaving the kitchen in total darkness. Natalie felt her heart jump then stutter before it began speeding. She strained to hear any sounds coming from the corner where she last saw Richard.

Pain exploded into white light when she felt the blow hit the side of her head.

Chapter Nineteen

Natalie woke up slowly, aware she had a bitch of a headache. Fucker hit her! Then she remembered witnessing both Beth's and Sarah's deaths and was overwhelmed with a sadness that made breathing difficult.

When she opened her eyes it was pitch-black and she started to panic when she couldn't see her hands in front of her face. She tried to sit only to hit her head and fall back.

What the—

She reached again and after a quick inspection, she was terrified to find she was trapped, and began to pound her fists on the wood, screaming for someone to let her out.

The fall hadn't killed Beth; Richard must have buried her alive. Natalie gasped, in her mind, the air was already gone and she started to choke. Natalie could smell the wet earth outside the box, could feel the splinters under her nails as she desperately tried to claw her way out of this vividly real nightmare. She kicked her feet and fought the space until the lack of oxygen affected her motor skills, slowing her down until finally, she lay still.

Van slammed back into her own house with a bang. After driving for three hours on her impulsive tangent, she'd parked outside Natalie's and stared at the dark windows and empty driveway for another forty-five minutes.

When had she become this irrational? Natalie had just come into her life, but Van was close enough to yesterday's memories of her cardboard half-life, that the thought of losing her already scared her. Telling herself it was all a simple misunderstanding didn't help smooth her agitation so she paced the floors until finally, some time later, she sat on the couch and willed the phone to ring.

When dawn broke and the early orange light filled her living room, Van realized she'd fallen asleep. After she started the coffee, she checked both of her phones, but there was no call from Natalie on either.

Anger started to burn under the hurt she was feeling. Since when did she put up with this shit? Van liked never having to explain herself; she did what she wanted, when she wanted. The hell with it, she thought. Natalie was off on a jealous huff on only another woman's word? How high school was that? It was an ugly reminder of why she avoided relationships. They didn't do anything but hurt in the end.

Van would work with the scheduled crew at Natalie's today so they could finish the job and she could get on with her life, without complications.

Such as it was.

Van was the first to arrive at Natalie's and immediately grabbed a shovel to dig out an area for the new fountain where the old one once stood. Maybe she could finish installing it before she arrived home and Van wouldn't have to see her at all. Hell with it, she didn't owe her any explanations, she hadn't done anything wrong.

The longer Van was there the more uneasy she became and she shivered in the early morning air. Van began digging in an effort to get her blood pumping. The physical labor warmed her but left her mind free to run. Who did Natalie think she was anyway, sneaking past her defenses? She didn't need her, Van didn't need anyone, she'd made certain of it.

She stomped the shovel into the dirt and the memory of Natalie crying in the rain came forward and hit her in the stomach. Just who was she trying to convince? She loved Natalie and would beg on her knees if she had to in order to get Natalie to listen. Van dug faster out of pure frustration, willing herself to work harder, not to think, and especially—not feel.

When her crew arrived, Van directed them to the trees that still needed trimming along the drive and various areas that needed prep work for the new plants and new sod that was to be arriving later in the afternoon.

Rick jumped in with her and they continued to dig until her back muscles screamed with the effort she used to swing her shovel. An hour later, he called "uncle" over his shoulder and climbed out of the hole.

"Christ, we digging to China or what?"

Van looked around. She had been so focused she hadn't realized how deep they were. She pulled herself up beside him and they trailed their legs into the space, resting for a minute.

She cast an eye over to the fountain. Five feet across, the bowl was shiny black granite with fluted edges. Rising from the center was a thick black stem, and at the top, three beautiful irises in full bloom from which streams of water would arc in graceful curves and return to the center. Natalie would love it. *Please come home.*

One of the guys came by and threw a couple of water bottles at them. Van took a long drink from the bottle and wiped the sweat from her forehead. Her critical eye found an uneven patch in the hole; she wanted the dirt perfectly level for the large granite base.

She jumped back in and picked up her shovel. The tip of the blade hit something solid, jarring her arms to her shoulder blades. She tried again with the same results. What the hell was it?

"We're going to get some lunch," Rick said.

Van rolled her eyes at him. If they only knew how haunted the house was, they'd never come back. "Go ahead." She waved him off. "We'll finish this afterward."

She walked around the side of the house and noticed a large hole with a pile of rocks by the back porch. "What's up with this?" she asked Leo.

"I was digging out the flower bed and ran into them. Do you think they were trying to shore up the foundation?"

"Could be. I'll take a look. Take your lunch break; we'll figure it out."

After he left, Van puzzled over the placement of the rocks, the foundation, and the position of the hole. Something was nagging at her conscious. She turned another stone and glimpsed wood. Her stomach sank and she quickly moved two more to reveal an old door that used to swing upward. Van found the handle and pulled; the aged wood crumbled in her grip then fell apart to reveal small stone stairs that led into the darkness.

The smell of mildew and ancient dirt hit her and she backed up a few steps. Van recalled Natalie telling her that Richard had locked Sarah in the root cellar. Now that she thought about it, these old houses usually had two entrances to the area, one accessible from the kitchen and another from outside.

She quickly ran back to her truck to get her flashlight and returned, praying she wasn't going to find what she thought she might. The air was stale and Van kept her breathing shallow, keeping the light directly in front of her as she descended the stairs.

She heard skittering noises around her and tried not to imagine what kind of spiders could make that sound. When she reached the bottom, she swept the small dank room with her light. It appeared to be completely empty but for a pile of rags in the corner. Van's body felt heavier with each step she took toward it, but she knew she had to see and crouched next to the small mound. Van blew to dislodge the loose dirt that settled on the surface, sneezing violently when it came back in her face.

When the dust settled, Van's scream lodged in her throat and she gagged. Two empty eye sockets stared back at her. She fell back on her ass, recovered herself, then quickly moved away from the skeleton, rushing back into the sunlight and fresh air.

Natalie shot straight up and gasped for breath, holding her chest as she wheezed in an attempt to draw clean air into her lungs. She saw her familiar bedroom furniture and heard the rhythmic ticking of the clock on her nightstand.

She covered her face with her hands and trembled; her nerves and system were shot. She was so done with these nightmares. A small lavender scented breeze washed over her.

"Hurry, love, we have to go."

"Sarah?" Natalie wanted to cry. Was she really awake or stuck in the past again? She looked at the clothes she put on before she went to bed and looked at the clock. Sun streamed in through the open window, and she knew it had been raining when she came home. Had she really been out for nearly twenty-four hours? She had to go to the bathroom.

Natalie felt sluggish and stiff when she came back out and stretched.

"He's coming."

Natalie twitched when she heard Sarah's whisper but couldn't see her. The crystal knob turned and her door swung open.

"Hurry!"

Van bent over with her hands on her knees and gulped air in an attempt not to throw up. When she felt the nausea pass, she went to the cooler to get another bottle of water and sat on the front porch stairs. Her hands shook, but she managed to call Rory and tell him what she found. He told her to stay away from the cellar; he would come check it out. What should she tell the crew that was due back any minute?

A strange car pulled up the drive and Van stared at the occupants and realized it was Natalie's mother in the driver's seat. She felt a rush of relief and rushed to the car to help her out. She assumed that the large man next to her was Natalie's father.

Colleen paled. "Her car isn't here. Where's my daughter?"

"She drove up to the city to deliver some paintings."

"Brian." Natalie's father said and shook Van's hand.

"Something's wrong. I can feel it." Colleen pointed at the house. "I found the connection—"

Van opened her mouth to tell her they had already found it and much more, but noticed the bedroom window was open. She was certain it was closed when she arrived that morning. Her stomach twisted painfully and she sprinted for the door.

Brian fumbled with the key. "It won't open."

Colleen snapped impatiently, "Well, jiggle it then."

"I *am* jiggling it, Colleen. It won't open."

Rather than jump into the conversation or do what she knew was worse, asking for a chance to work the key, Van went around the side of the house to the unlocked back door, trying not to think about the skeleton she'd found. She ran through the kitchen on her way to the front entry. She slipped on something and found herself flat on her back staring at the ceiling.

Van attempted to rise, but her legs went out from under her again. She looked at the floor and was shaken to see the puddle of blood. Bile rose to the back of her throat nearly choking her. "Natalie?" She slipped and slid her way to the front door, leaving bloody footprints in her wake. What happened in here? She was almost blind with terror when she reached for the handle and pulled.

"It won't open!" she yelled through the wood. She felt it shake and Brian told her to step back, he was going to kick it again. The door unlatched and swung open and he landed on the floor.

Van stood in the foyer, looked at Colleen, and began to hyperventilate. "Don't you see the blood?" It covered her clothes and she could see it dripping off the walls,

Natalie's father awkwardly gained his feet then patted her shoulder. "There's no blood here."

Oh God, she was losing her mind. "I swear there was a huge puddle of blood right there." Van pointed to where she slipped and fell. She turned a circle; the blood was gone, no traces remained.

The front door slammed and darkness fell around them. Several screams that seemed to come from every direction at once pierced Van's ears, and she heard Colleen gasp next to her.

She gripped her hand but couldn't say a word past the fear pounding in her throat.

A small orb appeared in the living room, increasing in size incrementally until Van could see Richard's image form and float cross-legged two feet above the floor. He opened his mouth and a high-pitched giggling filled the silence. The sound was horrible and Van could only liken it to the sound of fingernails on a chalkboard, grating on her nerves until she wanted to scream.

Colleen started to mumble, though Van couldn't tell if it were a prayer or an incantation. It was probably a little of both. Her blood turned to ice in her veins and she could only stare in disbelief at the apparition.

Richard looked at each of them, but his horrible gaze stopped at Brian. "You do have the look of Henry," he said. "He was a bit of a rake, you know. I paid off a few of his whores who claimed they carried his issue. Come here, son. Let me look at you."

Van looked at Brian. He was a little pale, but he wasn't cowering. "I'm not your son. I don't claim any part of you. What do you want?"

A strong wind rushed through the foyer and living room, carrying Richard to the second floor right before a door slammed upstairs.

Brian opened his mouth to say something but was interrupted by laughter that shook the window panes. The cold wind continued to whip around them and she shivered.

Van didn't even pause before she climbed. She took the stairs two at a time. When she got to the landing, the door to the third floor studio opened with a crash. She slowed and cautiously approached the door. The laughter stopped and the quiet was much more disturbing.

Natalie's parents caught up with Van. She stared into the dark entryway she knew should be streaming with light in the afternoon sun. She wasn't afraid to admit she was terrified of going any further.

She wanted to run in the opposite direction but climbed the stairs anyway to reach the top first. An old man rocked in a chair in the dim glow of a gaslight burning in the corner. He appeared much smaller; his face was so thin it looked almost skeletal through the paper thin skin stretched over his sharp cheekbones.

Now what was she supposed to do? What do you say to an insane ghost? Go home?

Richard stopped rocking and covered his ears. "Can't you hear them? They never shut up." He looked around the room, madness radiating from him. "They're laughing at me."

Van tensed when his horrible gaze settled on her. "Why don't you just go back to hell, Richard?" she snapped contemptuously. "Your parlor tricks are getting old."

"When will you learn that I am in charge here and that my word is law?" He began coughing, gasping for breath while he raised his hand weakly to point at Brian. "You are my legacy."

Brian stepped forward and thrust his face closer to the wheezing old man. "I ain't your jack. Get out of this house."

Richard appeared to grow older right before them, shrinking in size and demeanor. "You spawned another bitch that needs to be taught a lesson." He looked over their shoulders and his dark eyes spit hatred. "No, you can't make me leave. This is my house." He rubbed his claw hands together in glee. "But I taught her, didn't I?" Richard threw his head back and cackled. "I taught them all!"

"I found Sarah, you murderous asshole."

"What?" Colleen grabbed her arm. "Where?"

Richard's eyes glowed red and the wind picked up again until it reached gale force in the small room and nearly knocked Van off her feet. She saw Colleen hit her knees and crawl after a small glass vial that rolled across the floor. The windows blew open and over the howling rush, Van could hear shouting outside and remembered the returning crew and their orders to finish digging out the area for the fountain.

"It looks like a coffin!"

"No!" Richard bellowed to the men outside. "You can't have her. She's my property and she belongs here."

She knew in that instant that Beth's body had been found, but something was still nagging at her. *Think. Think.* The situation was out of control, and Van felt as if she were swimming through molasses. *Demons, skeletons, and what?*

The open window.

"Natalie!" she yelled then turned to run down the stairs.

Richard's head snapped around to look at her. He lifted a bony arm, pointed at her, and screeched.

She froze in mid-step and pain exploded in Van's head. She covered her ears then fell to the floor. She felt Brian cover her body with his own.

"You're weak, like my father!" Richard screamed at him. "She is not of your blood, but descended of a fucking servant bastard that my mother tried to pass off. She has no value."

Richard laughed and made a loose fist. "I can stop your heart. You are nothing," he said to Van. "Just like her." He tightened his bony fingers.

Van's chest constricted and lights danced in her vision then began to dim. Black butterfly wings fluttered frantically at the edge of her consciousness, then slowed.

And stopped.

Van felt a hand brush her cheek and she opened her eyes to the brightest light she had ever seen, pure, clean light that bathed her in warmth. She marveled at the hue of the grass under her and the flowers that bloomed in impossibly vivid colors she'd never come across before.

"Vanessa."

She turned her head toward the voice and her heart filled with joy.

"Mom?"

❖

Natalie was almost to the bedroom door when the house went dark. The door in front of her closed again, and she beat her fists against the wood. "Please let me out."

Raised voices from outside brought her attention to the window and she rushed over to scream for help. People were milling around a deep hole. Was that a police officer? The men were lifting something out.

"There's a skeleton in here!"

In the same instant, a boom shook the house and the floor buckled in waves under her feet. Screams sounded from upstairs and Natalie recognized her mother's voice. Natalie's adrenaline pumped so hard, she felt as if she flew to the door that opened instantly at her touch. Not stopping to wonder how, she reached the studio in time to see her mother throw something at Richard, who was—*oh God—*

solid in the room. Her mother was chanting in Latin; she recognized the language but didn't know the meaning of the words.

She noticed her father hunched over in the far side of the room. Natalie's vision narrowed to the jean-clad legs and familiar boots he huddled over. "No!" she screamed and tried to run, but her feet felt nailed to the floor and she couldn't move.

"You're too late!" Richard laughed. "Again." The laughter turned to a shriek when the water her mother was flinging sprayed over him, melting the flesh until it fell away to reveal a black skull. The jaw snapped open and closed with a horrible clicking sound.

A high-pitched keening wail filled the room and stabbed Natalie's nerve endings before it was abruptly cut off when Richard's skull fell off his neck and he disappeared.

The force that held her in place vanished, releasing her to run over to where her father was performing CPR on Van's body. "I've called the ambulance." Her mother said.

"No. No. No," Natalie cried while she dropped to her knees beside Van and patted her face. "Please come back. You can't leave me again." She saw the strain in her father's face then positioned herself so she could help.

Time stretched into an eternity while her father counted four compressions. He nodded to Natalie and she took a deep breath to give to Van. She felt a static shock where their lips touched.

One. Two. Three. Four. Breathe.

Again.

"Please, Van," she whispered. Van's lips softened beneath hers a split second before she opened her eyes. "Oh, thank God." Natalie was so relieved; she cried and laughed at the same time.

Her father leaned weakly against the wall and patted Van's shoulder. "Welcome back."

The turret windows shattered inward and Natalie screamed.

Maniacal laughter shook the walls and vibrated through the floor before Richard appeared again, showing no trace of the old man. Seven feet tall, he towered over them. "Oh, this is priceless. Did you really think it would be that easy? You stupid bitches *never* learn."

Natalie felt her hope draining away and hung her head. She didn't know what else to do. A red drop fell from her face onto her knee and then another.

The key.

The air compressed around her, making her sluggish and heavy, but she finally understood. She managed to grip a shard of glass in her numb fingers and slashed the sharp edge across her palm. "My blood."

Natalie looked at Van who was fumbling to get in her pocket. She handed the locket to Natalie before piercing her own hand.

"My blood," she said.

Richard stopped laughing.

Natalie's fingers were slippery, but she managed to open the catch and get the braided lock of hair across her palm before clasping it to Van's open hand. They raised their joined arms.

"Our blood."

"No. You can't do this!" Richard began to shake violently when a mist started to form behind him and quickly took shape. He tried to cringe away from it. "No!" he screamed. "Go away! I killed you both."

"Our blood," Beth and Sarah said together.

Natalie watched Richard shrink, his power stripped from him. He faded away while his cries echoed until finally, they grew fainter then stopped.

The room was hushed. Beth's face filled with love and she smiled gently. "Thank you."

Natalie's eyes were blurry with tears. She blinked to clear them.

Beth and Sarah were gone.

EPILOGUE

Van dropped a white rose then crouched next to the fresh hole. "Now you're home," she said. "Where you belong."

She stood straight, her chest filled with pride and love as each member of her family passed, covering the casket in the Easton family plot. Her father was last in line and pushed her grandfather's wheelchair closer.

Tears ran down her face when her father helped her grandfather stand and together, they placed the last roses on the coffin. Her grandfather said good-bye to the daughter of the fairy king and the princess who once lived in a tower.

Natalie cried softly beside her and Van tightened her arm around her shoulder.

"This was such a beautiful thing to do," Natalie said. "Burying them together."

Van dropped a kiss on her forehead. "She's family."

"Are you coming?" Van's father called over his shoulder.

"We'll meet you at the house," Van answered then turned to Natalie. "Could I have a few minutes?"

Natalie smiled. "Take your time."

Van held the last bouquet of flowers in her hand and walked a short distance down the path. She stopped in front of a marble headstone that already had fresh flowers at the base. Her throat tightened. Her father must have left them earlier in the day. She placed them anyway then sat, folding her legs under her.

The beauty of the day was all around her and she breathed in the warm summer air, savoring the scent. She thought of all the visits she'd made here over the years to visit her mother, then Cara.

Van no longer held any heavy grief in her heart. She knew they weren't really buried here in the ground. She smiled because she knew their spirits lived in a place so beautiful. Van knew it beyond description. They were happy and free. She'd seen it for herself.

If she closed her eyes, she could almost put herself there again. Almost. Oh, she still missed them, but she knew now that physical loss was only temporary. The people she loved never really went away.

They simply waited.

Van stood and brushed the grass off of her slacks. It was time to go home.

❖

Natalie opened the front door and smiled. The entire Easton family was inside, along with her parents. Food covered the table, laughing children were running up and down the hall, and everyone was talking at once, filling the home that had been empty of love for so long.

She was exhausted but strangely energized at the same time. Her mother laughed at something Van's uncle said and her father joined in. She was struck with that sense of homecoming she'd felt the first time she'd entered the house.

The afternoon sun streamed in the open windows. A single shaft of light lit the space above the fireplace where a new painting was hung just that morning. Natalie had painted the yard she'd seen in Beth's dreams.

Bold flowers bloomed and bright, beautiful colors seemed to leap from the canvas in a riot of hues. Larkspur feathered in beds behind bright pansies and rosebushes in full bloom. The original fountain sprayed with water depicted so realistically, the drops shimmered in the light. A picnic basket sat open, a bottle of wine and a loaf of French bread visible over the rim. A white-brimmed hat lay propped against the side. Beth sat in the grass in a lacy white dress, her legs tucked to one side. Her features, so like Natalie's own, depicted a look of pure adoration as she looked down at her hands hidden in the clouds of Sarah's dark hair spread about her lap. Sarah lay with her legs stretched out and feet crossed at the ankles. The painting appeared to have caught them in an intimate moment of love.

Natalie stood in front of the lovely scene and jumped when arms enclosed her from behind. She murmured in pleasure when she felt Van's hard body press against her back. She held the hands that crossed over her stomach, and they stood for a moment, rocking from side to side.

Van kissed the side of her neck and whispered in her ear. "You did a beautiful job. They look happy and crazy in love."

"They do. Finally."

"Come outside with me?"

They slipped out the back door and sat on the bench by the fountain. The sun felt so good, Natalie closed her eyes and tilted her face toward it, soaking in the warmth.

She was filled with a peaceful joy. This was her happy ending.

Natalie rested her head on Van's shoulder and looked at the pink scar across her hand. The permanent reminder of that afternoon.

She could recall staring into the empty space that held Beth and Sarah just a second before, hardly wanting to even dare to hope it was all finally over. Then she was in Van's strong arms, laughing and crying again while people stomped the stairs to surround them.

Van refused to let go of her while the paramedics checked them over. Natalie's father didn't have a scratch on him, but she and Van both had several that required stitches. They rode together to the hospital.

When Van began to explain what happened with Candy, Natalie stopped her. She didn't believe the lie anymore. Van had bled for her, for love.

There wasn't any magic stronger than that.

Natalie turned her hand so their scars were pressed together. "When I saw you on the floor, my heart stopped. All I could think of was that I would do anything, absolutely anything to get you back."

"It was your tears," Van said.

"My what?"

"I was talking to my mother's spirit and I felt your tears on my face. She told me I had a choice. I chose you."

Natalie kissed her softly. "I love you."

About the Author

No one ever clapped harder or louder than Yvonne Heidt did to keep Tinker Bell alive. When she was brought to a library at the age of six, she never looked back. She hardly ever meets a book she doesn't like and considered Jack London a personal friend while growing up. A fourth-generation San Franciscan, she lived for twenty years in the Puget Sound area of Washington State and is currently living in the South with her partner of over ten years, Sandy, and their four dogs. Writing is her passion, and she considers herself blessed beyond measure that she and her muse get along so well.

Books Available From Bold Strokes Books

Speed Demons by Gun Brooke. When NASCAR star Evangeline Marshall returns to the race track after a close brush with death, will famous photographer Blythe Pierce document her triumph and reciprocate her love—or will they succumb to their respective demons and fail? (978-1-60282-678-6)

Summoning Shadows: A Rosso Lussuria Vampire Novel by Winter Pennington. The Rosso Lussuria vampires face enemies both old and new and to prevail they must call on even more strange alliances, unite as a clan, and draw on every weapon within their reach—but with a clan of vampires, that's easier said than done. (978-1-60282-679-3)

Sometime Yesterday by Yvonne Heidt. When Natalie Chambers learns her Victorian house is haunted by a pair of lovers and a Dark Man, can she and her lover Van Easton solve the mystery that will set the ghosts free and banish the evil presence in the house? Or will they have to run to survive as well? (978-1-60282-680-9)

Into the Flames by Mel Bossa. In order to save one of his patients, psychiatrist Dr. Jamie Scarborough will have to confront his own monsters—including those he unknowingly helped create. (978-1-60282-681-6)

OMGqueer edited by Radclyffe and Katherine E. Lynch, PhD. Through stories imagined and told by youth across America, this anthology provides a snapshot of queerness at the dawn of the new millennium. (978-1-60282-682-3)

Coming Attractions: Author's Edition by Bobbi Marolt. For Helen Townsend, chasing turns to caring, and caring turns to loving, but will love take five steps back and turn to leaving? (978-1-60282-732-5)

Oath of Honor by Radclyffe. A First Responders novel. First do no harm…First Physician of the United States Wes Masters discovers that being the president's doctor demands more than brains and personal sacrifice—especially when politics is the order of the day. (978-1-60282-671-7)

A Question of Ghosts by Cate Culpepper. Becca Healy hopes Dr. Joanne Call can help her learn if her mother really committed suicide—but she's not sure she can handle her mother's ghost, a decades-old mystery, and lusting after the difficult Dr. Call without some serious chocolate consumption. (978-1-60282-672-4)

The Night Off by Meghan O'Brien. When Emily Parker pays for a taboo role-playing fantasy encounter from the Xtreme Encounters escort agency, she expects to surrender control—but never imagines losing her heart to dangerous butch Nat Swayne. (978-1-60282-673-1)

Sara by Greg Herren. A mysterious and beautiful new student at Southern Heights High School stirs things up when students start dying. (978-1-60282-674-8)

Fontana by Joshua Martino. Fame, obsession, and vengeance collide in a novel that asks: What if America's greatest hero was gay? (978-1-60282-675-5)

Lemon Reef by Robin Silverman. What would you risk for the memory of your first love? When Jenna Ross learns her high school love Del Soto died on Lemon Reef, she refuses to accept the medical examiner's report of a death from natural causes and risks everything to find the truth. (978-1-60282-676-2)

The Dirty Diner: Gay Erotica on the Menu, edited by Jerry L. Wheeler. Gay erotica set in restaurants, featuring food, sex, and men—could you really ask for anything more? (978-1-60282-677-9)

The Marrying Kind by Ken O'Neill. Just when successful wedding planner Adam More decides to protest inequality by quitting the business and boycotting marriage entirely, his only sibling announces her engagement. (978-1-60282-670-0)

Sweat: Gay Jock Erotica by Todd Gregory. Sizzling tales of smoking hot sex with the athletic studs everyone fantasizes about. (978-1-60282-669-4)

Missing by P.J. Trebelhorn. FBI agent Olivia Andrews knows exactly what she wants out of life, but then she's forced to rethink everything when she meets fellow agent Sophie Kane while investigating a child abduction. (978-1-60282-668-7)

Touch Me Gently by D. Jackson Leigh. Secrets have always meant heartbreak and banishment to Salem Lacey—until she meets the beautiful and mysterious Knox Bolander and learns some secrets are necessary. (978-1-60282-667-0)

Slingshot by Carsen Taite. Bounty hunter Luca Bennett takes on a seemingly simple job for defense attorney Ronnie Moreno, but the job quickly turns complicated and dangerous, as does her attraction to the elusive Ronnie Moreno. (978-1-60282-666-3)

Dark Wings Descending by Lesley Davis. What if the demons you face in life are real? Chicago detective Rafe Douglas is about to find out. (978-1-60282-660-1)

sunfall by Nell Stark and Trinity Tam. The final installment of the everafter series. Valentine Darrow and Alexa Newland work to rebuild their relationship even as they find themselves at the heart of the struggle that will determine a new world order for vampires and wereshifters. (978-1-60282-661-8)

Mission of Desire by Terri Richards. Nicole Kennedy finds herself in Africa at the center of an international conspiracy and is rescued by the beautiful but arrogant government agent Kira Anthony—but can Nicole trust Kira, or is she blinded by desire? (978-1-60282-662-5)

Boys of Summer, edited by Steve Berman. Stories of young love and adventure, when the sky's ceiling is a bright blue marvel, when another boy's laughter at the beach can distract from dull summer jobs. (978-1-60282-663-2)